# BLUE LINES & CHRISMUKKAH NIGHTS

## HOLIDAY SPARKS

EVEY LYON

# ASHER & GRACIE'S PLAYLIST

How to Dream by Sam Phillips

Santa Baby by Wolf Alice

Let it Snow by Kacey Musgraves

ACT! By Richy Mitch & The Coal Miners

Fade Into You by Mallrat

Eight Candles by Yo La Tengo

I Love You by two blinks, i love you

New Year's Day by Taylor Swift

Frosty the Snowman by Zee Avi

Sailor Song by Gigi Perez

Candlelight by The Maccabeats

Opaline by Novo Amor

Winter Wonderland by Bing Crosby

Spotless by Zach Bryan & The Lumineers

# CHAPTER 1
## ASHER

I refrain from stabbing the pumpkin-shaped butter, even though it's tempting. The fall season and especially Halloween are not for me. Kids in superhero costumes annoy me. And I don't have time for goblins and candy. It's the start of the hockey season, and we need to start strong. No distractions. I hate the marketing department when they steal one of my players away for a hot minute for some ridiculous social media post. The other day it was for our rookie to paint a pumpkin. Alas, hockey isn't only on the ice, which is why I'm sitting at the Dizzy Duck Inn in Lake Spark with the Spinners team owner and one of our major sponsors.

Charm. Obligation. And tableware and food saluting the autumn season in a small town.

That's my life right now.

I'm well aware that my name does not match the impression people have of me. Asher means "happy one" in Hebrew, and for the most part, I believe people see me as anything but. Not exactly grumpy, but determination can come off wrong.

"I'm glad that you're on board, Asher. I was getting

worried last season. The guys didn't seem the same," Hudson Arrows reflects as he cuts into his steak. Seems like a man who needs his protein supply, as he is in good shape for a guy the same age as my father. He's one of the major families in Lake Spark. For years he was one of the best coaches in professional football. Imagine the world's surprise when he decided he would sponsor a hockey team. But his reason is compelling; watching hockey was always his relaxing pastime, and now Lake Spark is his home.

Technically, we are a Chicago team, but we train a good distance outside of the city. It makes it easier to focus, to be honest. Small-town life mellows out the guys too. Maybe even me on occasion.

"They just needed a coach with new direction." Declan Dash grins at me. He is younger than Hudson but has kids in college. He's the team owner and used to play hockey himself. He lives and breathes our team.

I take a quick sip from my glass of wine. "We still have work to do, but there is only one way to go." No shit we have a lot of work to do. Their former coach had no strategy, always changed plays and lines, and couldn't be professional in any press conference. The team was fed up, which means a few unrestricted free-agent players escaped over the summer, and the coach was fired. The former coach left nothing posi- tive in his trail except the job opportunity for me.

"That's the spirit." Hudson smiles.

Thankfully dinner hasn't been miserable. Hudson and Declan are laidback and invested. It's just that I could use the downtime to gear up for the next two away games. I didn't want to stay with the expansion team in northern Wisconsin, and being closer to my parents in Chicago was appealing. Plus, teams that are used to not doing well tend to see a light at the end of the tunnel eventually, and then the thirst to win is unstoppable. That's why I'm with the Spinners.

"It will be great at the team Halloween party. Seeing the guys with their kids is always a laugh. I forget if we are doing the puppy adoption booth this year. They normally use those photos for the holiday calendar." Declan is so damn happy that it nearly causes the corner of my mouth to stretch an inch.

Nearly.

"I'll take off my coach's hat, I promise." I'm only half joking, but he probably doesn't realize. I don't hear his reply because my eyes have latched on to a woman who just entered the restaurant.

Sure, she is probably a little younger than me, late twenties maybe to my forty but age has never been a deterrent to me. Long legs highlighted by a mocha-colored dress, light brown hair that falls to just below her breasts, which are perfectly pert and full. I sense that her smoky brown eyes that latch on to mine are dangerous, an instinct of mine. I've seen her a few times before at hockey events.

It's only a brief moment until we lose the connection, but she walks with purpose straight to our table, which has me wildly curious. She arrives with a friendly smile before leaning over to hug Hudson.

"Hey, Daddy."

*Ah*, his daughter.

The man looks elated by this surprise. "Why am I so lucky today to see my beautiful daughter? This is my daughter Gracie," Hudson quickly mentions to me.

"Or just Grace because I'm no longer a child," she humorously reminds her father. She gives Declan a friendly nod hello before her eyes land on me, not even blinking, and she gives me the once-over real quick before turning her attention back to her father. "Mom said you would be here, and I wanted to say hi, as I have a yoga class at the spa next door."

For some reason, everything about that sentence is ripe with privilege. I have visions of her being spoiled and having life handed to her on a silver platter.

"You've met our new coach, right?" Declan directs his assumption to Gracie.

"I have not. But the team actually won a game recently, so I figured that we probably have a new coach." Her sass is a little brazen, but Declan seems to be used to it and only chuckles.

Me? My brows rise from her candor.

Hudson clears his throat. "Excuse my daughter. Her humor is from... I'm not sure which side of the family."

I smirk smugly at her when her lashes flutter at me. "No apologies needed. At least she acknowledges a win."

"It was one. I think you still have about eighty more games this season before we can throw the confetti." Her fire is refreshing.

"Gracie," her father mutters her name as a warning.

Declan just chuckles under his breath. "She reminds me of the days she would babysit Willow, my daughter, and she would be a protective wolf at the playground. A little ruthless with the parents, too."

Her eyes narrow in on me for a few seconds, as if she is pinning me to a bulletin board, right before she slides her gaze back to her father. "I really just wanted to stop by. The cons of being an adult is I don't live under your roof and get to see you every day. Also..." She winces. "Mom kind of sent me here to remind you that she's contemplating inviting the rabbi over for Hanukkah this year, and even though it's only October, he's in popular demand, so we need to get ahead of the line."

Hudson's face completely falls in a humorous way. "I thought we were going all-in on Christmas this year?"

She shrugs. "Take it up with the missus. I'm just the cute messenger." Her voice is floaty.

Grace and her dad begin to chat about something while Declan grabs my attention when he leans into my space. "How is it with your cousin on the team?"

"He's my second cousin, and it makes no difference," I clarify. Tyler Ives is only somewhat related to me. His mother's brother is married to my aunt. Tyler is younger than me by a few years, so we never grew up close. He's at least a solid player, and as such, I'll treat him like one. Same with my little brother Shaw who also plays hockey. He's on a team out in California, and when we play against them, then he is my opponent, not a relative.

My eyes drift back to Grace, and maybe and that's the reason Declan leans in a little closer to me. "We keep our sponsors happy. We don't go near certain things that might not make sponsors happy. Got it?" he warns me with a low voice and a tight smile on his face.

*Translation:* Stop eye-fucking the woman at the table who is feisty and gives me the feeling that she would probably be in agreement with every scenario in my head that involves no clothes.

I throw him an agreeing smile. "Of course. The focus is the team, and we will bring home a cup this season."

He pats my shoulder. "That's what I love to hear."

We both return our attention to Hudson and Grace who are ending their conversation. She gives us a goodbye too before dashing off. A little disappointment pings inside me because I think I wanted to experience more of her banter or simply admire the gleam in her eyes that would for a brief few seconds get caught in my gaze.

I'm quick to bury the last few minutes away in my head and return my focus on my steak and the conversation about the league's latest gossip and an explanation about the local holiday traditions. The holiday market a few towns over in Everhope is apparently worth a visit if I actually ever decide to be social on my seldom days off. I'm a people person, I have to be with what I do. It's just there are very few days off during the season, and I need to refuel my engine.

As we wait for a round of scotch, I excuse myself and go to the men's room, but when I turn the corner in the hall, I nearly run into someone.

"Sorry." I'm quick to steady the arm of the woman in an oversized sweater and yoga pants, only to realize when my eyes flick up that it isn't just any woman. It's *her*.

Grace straightens her posture, only for a smirk to slowly draw on her lips, glossy with a fresh layer of balm, and I notice because she makes no effort to step back, nor do I. "You again. Mr. Saving the Team."

"Someone has to do it." I'm not going to win the fight to control my cocky smirk.

I'm sensing playfulness, it's a sort of vibe she emits. "You know." She leans against the wall and crosses her arms. "I have a theory about you."

"What would that be?"

"You think I'm just a daddy's girl. First impressions and all."

She's not exactly wrong. "How intuitive of you." I keep my face stoic.

"But it's quite hypocritical, since you are Asher Tate, the son of Cole and Ruby Tate. You were not exactly struggling on your road to success."

This woman. Is she part devil?

Instantly, I'm offended, as it's a sore spot. "Just because my dad is floating in cash from his little investment empire, I assure you that his ability to step on the ice is non-existent, and I had to work just as hard as anyone to land a spot on the college team, then be to be drafted and play pro for a few years. And last year? You know, coaching a team that actually made it to the playoffs? Yeah, that's all me, princess," I bite back.

It only causes her to grin. "Touchy."

I roll my eyes and internally remind myself of Declan's words, but this woman pulls at me in every miserable yet enticing way, and we've only just met. "How is it going with your life? Out from under mommy and daddy's thumb? Or still playing messenger so you can see your parents every day?"

She doesn't flinch an inch. "Life is going perfectly, thank you. I will not apologize for my mother owning a beautiful lingerie company or that she has taught me the art of designing and creating dresses. A profession passed down generations. Tradition and all." Grace seems completely comfortable and confident with her belief. Proven by the fact that she pretends to evaluate her nails.

The confidence is refreshing. She's on my level, and it's compelling to see, which is why I ease and tone down my smirk as our eyes lock. "Seems we might have things in common then."

"Hardly. I have a feeling that I get more excited for the team Halloween party than you."

"It's the start of the holiday season, what's not to love?" I'm sarcastic. Halloween rolls into weeks of crunchy leaves and pumpkin lattes and all the crap that people say they love. Then comes Thanksgiving, and the family doesn't back off for the next six weeks. There are too many holidays between now and January.

Hey eyes squint, and she seems to be studying me, and I return the look. "Yes?" I wonder.

"Nothing. It's just… I'm sensing you actually have a soft spot for Christmas."

I sigh and shake my head as I lean my back against the wall with my hands stuffed in my pockets and my ankles crossed, our proximity still far too close. "I'm like you from what I heard at the table. It's Chrismukkah in my family."

"Ah." Her smile is genuine. "What's the divide? Mom or dad?"

"Hanukkah is from her side, and my dad is all Christmas. Some years they go crazier for one over the other."

She clucks her tongue. "My mom too. I'm named after her grandmother. Ruth is my middle name. Normally my dad and mom flip a coin because even when we do both holidays, it feels like one always prevails over the other. This year, I don't think they even tossed a coin, it's more that she isn't even religious, yet heard the local rabbi is going through a divorce, and she thought of presenting that option to me. It's totally fine. He's one of those liberal Judaism guitar-playing kind of guys. Trying to relate to the younger crowd. Could have potential." I sense that her wit is out, and I find it funny.

"You sound convinced," I say, playing along.

She wiggles her finger at me. "Trust me, it would probably be more bearable than if I brought home a hockey player. That would be an intense holiday dinner. Sometimes, I'm convinced my dad is a secret agent because his interrogation skills are top notch. It was hell when I was a teenager."

"Should he have been worried?"

Grace fakes a gasp. "Of course not. I was a perfect straight-A student who most definitely never ever ditched a class at Lake Spark Academy to hang out with the quarterback on the football team."

I chuckle because she is a character, that's for sure. "Is that why there is a memo that every guy from the team should stay outside a ten-mile radius of you and Willow?"

Her eyes blaze open. "Is there?" Her face screws up. "Because for Willow, the owner's daughter, I know there is. Declan would get that player traded faster than you could sneeze."

"Fair enough."

We both give the older man walking by a mere glance before our sight darts straight back to each other. "Anyhow. You can warn your wife that the Halloween party is the start of holiday hell for most of us. But hey, if there are no puppies, then at least there are decorative cookies."

"No wife or girlfriend," I clarify bluntly.

She brings her hands together and near to her chest. "Oh, really?" She fakes shock. "I was getting concerned about five sentences back that I was flirting too much when my conscience hit me. Then I remembered that I should probably double-check a fact that I already suspected."

I chortle a laugh and can't help the grin that I shouldn't be sporting. "I would say that I should be concerned about every word in that sentence, but…" The way the corner of her mouth is etched with a shade of a gentle smile draws me in. "I guess I'm not," I softly answer.

She hums a sound.

I lift a finger into the air. "You know, you really are a Gracie instead of a Grace. You are too bubbly and playful to be just a Grace."

Her brows lift. "I'm also not five with piggy tails, so nicknames are not needed."

"Too bad. I'm calling you Gracie."

Her eye roll is classic but suits her. "So be it. Nobody listens to me anyway."

For a second, we both stand there in a moment that feels like an October breeze. Refreshing yet there are unsettling leaves that blow around.

There is something about Gracie that feels like she is causing chaos in the air around me. That's probably why I can't seem to shake my thoughts and force myself to step back, instead opting for our stare to linger and my eyes to drop down to her lips.

I'm a guy with needs, and sometimes you need a no-strings-attached night. Yet, every alarm in my head has me screaming that she is trouble and I should walk away.

One of us breaks the moment, and I can't even say who. "Well, you should get back to your little meeting."

"I should," I agree.

After a long moment, I finally move. She has the same thought, and we nearly run into one another. Our feet shuffle, but we keep moving to the same side.

"Oh, sorry," she apologizes, but there is no need. I just got an opportunity to orbit closer to her body that radiates warmth, the smell of roses wafting in the air. And when we finally move in opposite directions, we both pause.

"Seems our feet have different ideas," I comment. Because my thoughts involve inappropriate behavior.

Her eyebrow rises, and I realize that she might have picked up on my less-than-honorable thoughts. Maybe that is why she seems entertained.

Clearing my throat, I move us past that. It's been a fun few minutes, but I have a team to manage and no distractions to be had.

We both give the faintest of smiles for our goodbye. "See you around, Coach," she rasps in passing as she walks away with a sway to her hips. I don't even think it's forced, she is just a natural tempting creature.

My jaw flexes side to side as I take a moment for myself.

I know one thing for sure. At tomorrow's practice they are going to catch hell, because I need to work out some frustration that I didn't get to touch the woman currently walking away.

# CHAPTER 2
## GRACIE

Zipping up my purse, I sling the strap over my shoulder. My mom is in the corner of the boutique, busy comparing material swatches against one another, and I'm not even sure she notices that I'm about to leave. She's in her zone. Piper Arrows is a vision of elegance. I hope to have received her genes when I get older, down to her thick hair that still falls below her shoulders. Not many women can pull that off with age. She is also quite a bit younger than my dad.

"I'm going to head out, I promised to meet Lainey," I say as I approach the door.

"Have fun." She doesn't even glance up as her concentration remains.

The corner of my mouth snags to form a smile because she is just talent and kindness all rolled into one.

I've learned from the best, and I'm in love with working on my current creations—dresses with a sophisticated classic feel. I also have new design software that I'm getting the hang of. Still, I prefer my little notebook of sketches. It's part of the tradition. My mother and late-great-grandmother have passed down the ritual, whether they intended to or not. My great-grandmother arrived from Europe and worked her way up from seamstress to a woman with a designer label, and she would carry around her journal when observing people. Many would assume I've gone the easy route and stayed in the family business, considering my mom is already established with Piper Ginger, partly named after her. But you can't fake design ideas. Plus, we have a different style, and I'm still learning in some ways.

Closing the door behind me, I can still hear the bell jingle above the door. Taking a few steps toward the corner of the street, I glance down while I tie the belt of my oversized sweater.

Suddenly, I feel a strong bump against my shoulder because someone else just plowed into me.

"Sorry," we say in unison as we both steady our footing.

My eyes scrape up because it's that masculine voice that sears through every tingle inside of me. I'm met with the vision of dark hair, and his whiskey-brown eyes are electrifying, lit today with a flare because of recognition, but I swear I notice something more sinister. He could strip me naked with only his gaze.

"We meet again." Asher smirks lightly. He's standing before me with dry cleaning draped over his shoulder and his fingers wrapped around the hook.

I blink twice, and a light switch is flipped inside of me. My brows shoot up, and I feel my own smirk crawl on my face. "So it seems." It lingers in the air because neither one of us looks away, and the brief silence feels as though we are testing the waters. I'm not even sure for what.

"Not planning your wedding with the rabbi?" he teases.

I smile that he remembers. "Nah, he doesn't know how to use a stick, so that's a no-go." His eyes grow wider. "A hockey stick," I clarify, but I enjoy that his mind just went off track.

The instant attraction is concerning, the way it takes over my entire body. It's overpowering. That is exactly why I tear my gaze away. "You're carrying dry cleaning." My jaw goes slack.

Asher's face squinches. "Why do you make it sound as though it's strange."

I shrug. "I don't know. I just kind of assumed you would have someone do that for you. An assistant, housekeeper, though we established there is no girlfriend, so that option is off the list."

His smirk morphs into a grin, and I'd like to think that he is enchanted by me. "Well, I wear a lot of suits for games, and I am a normal forty-year-old man who can manage errands just fine."

My lips stretch a line. "Forty. Good to know."

"As opposed to your…" he preambles.

"Twenty-seven… I'm twenty-seven." I smile.

"Good to know." He cranes his neck and skims his eyes over my shoulder. "That's where you work?"

I follow his line of sight and land on the boutique. "Yes. That is where the magic happens," I proudly answer. His mouth opens but then snaps closed. I squint my gaze to get a better read on his mind. Then it hits me. "The design magic."

"Right," he voices tightly. "Interesting displays."

Looking back, I notice my mother staring through the window with a puzzled face, only to shake her head to herself and return to her task at hand. It isn't her that Asher notices, though.

"Can't handle a little black lace and stockings?" I ask. The mannequin displays a classic collection, the type of lingerie that never goes out of season. The holiday-focused display will go up next week.

He clears his throat. "No. I can handle that just fine. But since I'm a man of honesty, then I will admit that seeing that and you in the same vision is a little…" He tips his head gingerly to the side.

My eyes widen as I patiently wait for the end of his thought. I even smile flirtatiously. "What?" I say, goading him.

"I'm a gentleman today, so I shall not answer."

I nibble on my bottom lip and almost blush. Luckily, I can get a grip of situations. "Manners get you far. With the holidays coming up, you'd better be nice." I wiggle a finger at him.

"We still have Halloween before I need to worry about Santa's naughty list," he deadpans.

"Exactly. Only nice boys get candy when trick-or-treating."

He drags his strong hand across his tight jawline. "I'm going to pretend you meant nothing by that. I ensure people avoid the penalty box on a daily basis. I would consider that a point for the nice list."

My hand lands on my tipped-out hip. "Depends. Did you smile at the dry cleaner?" I fake seriousness.

"Yes. Any more questions? I sense this conversation is taking an odd turn."

Shrugging, I blow out a breath. "It seems so. That is why I'm going to head along." I cluck my tongue.

He steps to the side. "Sure. Anyway, have a good day."

"You too." I smile politely in passing.

Even walking away, I feel a heavy set of eyes watching me. I can't help wondering what he is thinking.

Le sigh, we both have things to do today.

THROWING a few bags of bite-size chocolate bars into my cart, my best friend Lainey follows suit.

"You're more than welcome to join us for Halloween," she reminds me before blowing her sun-kissed lock of hair away from her eyes. Lainey is a single mom to her son, Enzo, which means trick-or-treating in the damn cold. Her brother used to live here but moved to play hockey for another team.

"I'm good. I'm just going to hand out candy, turn the light off early, and relax on my couch. Maybe I'll work on some designs."

Halloween isn't for a few days, but I already have my relaxing plan in place.

"I'm envious," Lainey comments.

We continue our stroll down the aisle at the superstore near the highway. "No, you are not. You love Enzo to the moon and back."

The type of smile only reserved for her son breaks out. "I do. One day maybe you will experience the same type of love."

I lift a shoulder, as I've only thought about having kids once or twice. Right now, I've been focused on my dress designs and getting my feet on the ground for making a name for myself.

Changing topics, I can't help but tease her. "Still want to strangle your neighbor?"

Dread fills her face. "Ugh, don't remind me." That was slightly unconvincing which is exactly why I do remind her.

"Why don't you ask Tyler to go trick-or-treating with you?"

She swipes a plastic witch decoration off the shelf into her cart. "He has hockey. They have a game or practice. It's the universe telling me that I shouldn't have to put up with his company." He plays for the Spinners and is actually quite talented.

"So that's a 'no, Gracie, we won't be going to the next game so I can watch him skate and hope his jersey ends up on my floor,'" I tease her.

She playfully shoves me as we turn the corner. "Don't be annoying. If I go to a game, it's because the Spinners are actually worth a ticket these days."

"Probably because of the new coach who wears a suit well." Asher definitely has left an impression on me. Every word he speaks is on my level. It feels like we share the same thoughts that are completely rewarding to my imagination.

It's true, I might have watched an extra game on TV just to see him coaching from the bench. I just wasn't going to admit that earlier when I ran into him. Men in suits who cause my nipples to peak purely from words alone deserve my attention, including screen time.

Lainey pauses for a second to think. "I guess he is kind of easy on the eyes. Kind of the older yet still young, so he looks good in a suit kind of vibes."

"He's kind of suave yet cracks a smile in a warm way. I mean, he's probably even better with his clothes off." I have no problem owning my thoughts or views. Being blunt has always come naturally to me. My dad says I take after my great-grandmother in that department.

Lainey chuffs a laugh. "Does he not have a wife or girl-friend? Because if he doesn't, then that right there is a red flag. He isn't a bad catch."

I study the sale on laundry detergent on the display at the end of the aisle as we slowly stroll. "Single."

"How do you know?"

I smirk to myself at the encounter we shared. "I've run

into him twice now, and we spoke. He was at dinner with my dad the other week and we ran into one another in the hall. Then earlier today, outside of the boutique. For someone we all assume is uptight, he has a loose button or two."

Her eyes pop out as she stills. "Someone is smitten."

Rolling a shoulder back, I'm aware that the guy has a pull. "Sometimes flirtation comes naturally between two people," I justify. Besides, I haven't been with someone in over a year.

"Maybe."

"I'm fairly confident that if the team loses a game, then Asher is completely unleashed in the bedroom," I say without thought.

She bubbles a laugh. "Filtered that thought much?"

"What?" My voice rises an octave. "I notice these things. Sex is a very natural human instinct, and we don't need to wait for Mr. Right to enjoy it."

My friend blows out a breath. "True. I'm just trying not to picture it. I prefer to keep the photos with hockey players painting pumpkins in my head. Did you see them?" Lainey pulls out her phone, swipes, then hands it to me. "You are going to regret that you didn't make it to the team party."

Probably. My dad is always invited, and normally I tag along, but I wanted to help my older brother, Drew, with his kids since his wife was out of town.

I skim the photos on the social media feed. Hockey players painting a scary pumpkin, hockey players painting a superhero pumpkin, hockey players painting a referee pumpkin, and a hockey coach with a feigned smile painting a ghost pumpkin.

"He looks like he doesn't want to be there," I observe and swipe more photos, then stall on one. "And now he most definitely appears like he doesn't want to be there." Asher has a pirate hat on and an inch of a forced smile. That is until the next picture where he cracks when someone hands him a Labrador puppy that needs to be adopted. An honest smile looks good on him. I tip my head to the side a smidgen as I study him. "Well, this photo is…"

"Fire emoji, wink, fire emoji, pepper, heart, fire emoji? Yeah, the post comments answered that thought for you."

I chuckle as I hand her phone back. "I mean… the guy has looks. Worth another chat, too. If the opportunity arises, I might as well allow fate to run its course," I reply nonchalantly.

She chuckles. "Lucky him."

"Maybe."

Fantasies are safer, though.

# CHAPTER 3
## GRACIE

There is something cozy about Main Street in Everhope on a fall evening. There is an abundance of haystacks and pumpkin decorations around town and the occasional scarecrow where a shop owner got creative. Outside of Foxy Rox, the coffee spot in town, they have a scarecrow sitting on a hay bale with a to-go coffee cup. Some people use white decorative lights, which is smart because they can keep them up for the rest of the holidays this year.

I'm not one for ghosts and goblins, but more refined autumn colors and elegant decorations. I mean, maybe when I was younger, I got a little festive during the holiday. You can't exactly go wrong dressing as a cheerleader with fake blood on her head. But now, I'm older and appreciate a little more subtlety when it comes to the Halloween costume.

However, right now, with sleet on an October night, it suddenly feels like a horror film. I hate that I need to hold up an umbrella because it means that I can't hold my coat tighter around my body. They say it's going to be this way all night. Typical Illinois, unpredictable. Snow in October isn't that rare, and I've heard it indicates many omens when it does happen. Who knows what this year's omen is.

There are a few people walking on the other side of the street who are using their coats as cover as they dash into a new wine bar in town. The beep of a car unlocking and the flash of lights right in front of me draws my attention up, from staring at the dusting of white melting on the ground to the man running to the sports car, but as he opens the door, he flicks his gaze up, with his eyes striking my own before he does a double take and his gaze holds onto me.

"Gracie?"

That voice. It's familiar. Already something bounces above my bellybutton, I guess excitement.

I hurry a few steps to get a better look, and the streetlights give enough brightness. It doesn't take long to confirm what I thought. "Asher?" I sound just as surprised as him.

He shuts his door and circles around the car to me. Luckily my umbrella is big enough that he can join me under it, and it helps that he grabs the handle so he can hold it over us in a better position as he towers over me, except now his deep cologne with a hint of pine invades my air.

"You have a thing for running into me."

His free hand swipes across his chiseled jaw. "Who says it's me. You could be stalking me for all I know."

The corner of my mouth twists from the smirk fighting to spread. "Should I be concerned that *you're* stalking *me*?"

"Not my style. You should consider yourself lucky. They say third time is the charm, which means you're getting the best version of me right now. What are you doing here?" he wonders.

"I live in Everhope. You?"

"I was having dinner at the River Bell with one of the assistant coaches who lives nearby."

We look at one another in slight disbelief. The odds of running into one another in this county are high, but still, when it happens, it's pleasant... okay, a gift.

"Ah yes, I remember how you enjoy evening work dinners."

His head tips slightly to the side. "Dinner is over. I'm on my way home."

"The River Bell is a nice restaurant." It's on an old steamboat.

"It was pretty good. Can't go wrong with roast chicken, I guess. So, you live in Everhope?" he repeats. Even with the sound of a car driving against the wet pavement, I can hear he is still slightly puzzled at this coincidence.

Speaking up, I explain. "Yeah, gives me a little space from my parents and the boutique in Lake Spark. I have a friend who lives here, too."

His smirk feels unsafe. "Makes sense. Lake Spark isn't so far. A few of the guys on the team live around here."

Lightning followed by a boom startles us both. I peek out from the cover of the umbrella to get a view of the sky, and even though it's dark, I see the outline of clouds when another lightning strike flashes before I return under the umbrella. "I hate October storms in Illinois. They are cold, and then comes this weird sort of rain but not rain kind of snow."

"We call that sleet," he deadpans.

I give him a side glare. "Har-har." We both stop our wide grins and realize that here we are again. "Besides, safety first. I don't think you are supposed to have an umbrella up if there is lightening."

"That would be a tough decision. Chance of getting elec-trocuted or guaranteed getting wet?"

My mouth instantly gapes, and my eyes blaze from his

words. Everything inside of me coils in the best possible way, a tightness in my belly and my chest beginning to pound. "Wow."

He chuckles under his breath because he understands that his sentence was open to interpretation. "The rain. I mean the rain," he says sincerely, yet there is still mischief in his eyes, the streetlight highlighting his gleam.

I hate this attraction suddenly. It's overbearing and magnetic. And what are the chances that we cross paths at this moment.

"To even the awkward conversation happening. *Maybe*, I can say that you were wearing a dark gray suit at yesterday's game." I have no problem admitting that I turned my TV on.

His head retreats, slightly astonished. "Needed something to look at?"

I shrug and play casual. "I mean, might as well reap the benefits of a winning hockey team. If you get ejected like the last coach and swear while you stomp on the bench, then that will really make my week, if you feel so inclined."

Flirting is good for the soul, and it seems to come naturally to us.

His deep chuckle wraps around my core. "I have a feeling that your mind could get us both in trouble."

Stepping closer to him, my confidence causes me to feel that it is the right thing to do. I consider myself sexy no matter where I am or what I'm wearing. I have poise. "You would only think that if you knew where a dirty mind could go," I whisper.

His eyes peer down, and his intense stare pierces mine. "Touche. I should probably go before we both find ourselves in trouble."

"Good luck with that. The weather isn't ideal. Sometimes the road between Everhope and Lake Spark can flood, and the detour goes through duck territory where you end up waiting half an hour for a family of ducks to cross the road. It's night-time, so the deer decide they are fearless and just stand in the middle of the road, unwilling to move. Don't get me started on the foxes around here."

His tongue slides to the corner of his mouth, and his face remains a stoic slyness. "I would have to be careful anyways. If I'm around you, something tells me that it's just as dangerous."

I swear he steps a smidgen closer to me, our bodies almost brushing. The touch would fill the void of this static tension between us. But just as I make my move, cold water lands on me, and I yelp.

It comes from the side, which means the umbrella doesn't save me. Looking over my shoulder, I see that a little boy is following his parents and stomping into puddles in the process. He would be a little rascal, except his unruly behavior means I've fallen forward and straight into Asher's hard body.

His free hand steadies my arm, and I freeze. It's not even from the cold water. It's because I get that touch I've been seeking, but only because Asher holds my arm in concern, his hands feeling strong. "Yikes. You okay?"

I peer up, only to find his own eyes dipped down to watch me. Everything feels heavy between us still.

I reluctantly glance behind me to see my jeans completely soaked. "It will be fine, just cold."

"Where's your car?" He slowly lets me go.

"Parked up the street, but it doesn't matter, I live up here." I point to a few buildings up ahead.

His eyes grow big and his nose lifts. "Really?" Not my imagination, that sounds promising.

"Yeah, uh… do you want a coffee or tea?" I try to avoid

the view of his facial expression, instead focusing on the street, and in the corner of my eye, I notice that he has done the same. We both observe the sleet turning into giant watery snowflakes. "It will probably stop a little later." Our eyes latch at the same moment.

He smiles tightly and scratches his cheek, debating with himself, and I find it amusing. "That is…"

"Tempting, I know." I finish his sentence in good humor.

We hear the sound of the music and patrons from the wine bar in the background when someone opens the door while he thinks for a second. "Okay."

My grin is satisfied, but my body is heightened from his presence.

He begins to wrestle with the umbrella. "I think I choose rain. I can't risk the lightning accident."

I laugh. "The statistics of that are slim, you know."

Closing the umbrella, he shrugs as we are left standing in the rain. "Fuck, this was a bad idea."

"Not going to argue. Come on."

Indicating with my head, I motion for him to follow me.

MY LOFT APARTMENT is in an old building with a specialty wine store downstairs. My place is by no means a mansion, but all of the fixtures have been updated and the ceilings are high. The place feels like a home.

We race under the door's overhang and let out a sigh, mixed with wide smiles on our faces. I stomp my shoes on the mat before leaning down to the plant by the doormat, and I lift the pot and swipe out my key.

Asher touches my arm. "What the hell?"

"What? I forgot my key, so I'm using the spare."

"Anybody could find that and break in." He sounds both shocked and protective, and that isn't helping my heightened senses.

I stand with the key between my fingers and pretend to think about it. "Nope. All good. This is Everhope. The entire Lake Spark County actually, the crime rate is like nada. I mean, the last time a security alarm went off in this town, it was because a goat got loose and broke into someone's kitchen. Actually, it was going after a bowl of Halloween candy, or was it Thanksgiving pumpkin pie. I don't remember," I ramble.

His mouth opens, but he gives up his rebuff.

Opening the door, we both walk in and up the stairs. We leave our wet coats on the hooks and the umbrella by the side. He trails behind me as we enter my home.

"Tea, coffee, wine, magic potion for the sake of Halloween?" I offer the list.

"Tea is fine."

I glance over my shoulder, questioning if I heard him right. I turn and walk backwards as he follows me. "I was not expecting you to say that. It's so… I'm not sure, but it's hard to imagine someone so… drinking tea. I mean, no offense, but you seem kind of cold and heartless to many. Yet, you drink a cup of tea."

"It's detoxing."

"Okay. Will lemon ginger work then?"

"Sounds good."

"Perfect. It pairs excellently with the piece of Halloween candy that you'll get if you're nice."

"I'm never nice," he replies flatly.

"And that's what the world likes about you." I spin on my heel when I get to the kitchen, and Asher straggles behind in the living room. It's open plan, which means conversation can carry on.

My hands are busy preparing the water, but I notice Asher perusing my living room, pausing when he sees the framed photographs on my side table.

"Who is this?" he asks and holds up a photo in a frame.

I smile instantly and abandon the kettle that I just set on the stove to join and study the photo with him. "That's my brother, Drew." I was younger in the photo, probably around three.

He scoffs a laugh. "What? He's like the same age as your mom."

"Yeah, he's my half-brother. We have the same dad. You would think it would be kind of awkward at every family dinner, but we just never say stepmom and then it's fine. He married a Blisswood, so he lives not far in Bluetop and helps with their winery when he isn't constructing things." Everyone knows about the Olive Owl brand.

Asher seems interested and meets my eyes for a beat when he sets the frame down.

I point to the next one. "That's my great-grandmother. She died when I turned ten. A fiery woman. Hysterical, too."

"That explains a lot." His comment is flippant.

He seems like a tough cookie, but also, there is a glimmer in his eyes that makes me believe it's for show and he is toying with me.

"I'm honored if I take after her, although my dad is 100% convinced that she haunts him every time he makes a non-traditional choice." He huffs out a laugh because I sound serious, and I am. "No joke. When I didn't have a Bat Mitzvah, he couldn't sleep for weeks. Then one Eastover, when he had an Easter egg hunt for everyone before Passover dinner, suddenly this clock on the wall just *poof*." I gesture with my hands. "Just dropped to the floor and broke for no reason."

His eyes squint and his face screws up. "Your family is interesting."

I pat his shoulder. "And I'm sure yours isn't."

He whistles and grins. "That explanation is for another day."

"Well, it's another day, so spill." I motion for him to join me in the kitchen, and he obliges.

He perches on the stool at the kitchen island while I return to my task of making tea.

"My parents are loving. My dad is ruthless when it involves business but completely turns soft if it involves his kids. He came to every hockey game growing up, even though he probably wishes I played football—"

I interrupt as the kettle on the stove begins to whistle. "My father would happen to agree."

"Right. You must have been to your fair share of football games growing up with your dad."

I nod proudly as I pour the water over the bags in each mug. "Yes. But he also tried to keep me out of the public eye so I could live a normal life. And tell me about your mom?"

"My mom is a free spirit who will photograph anything. I also have a little brother."

I interrupt. "Yeah, also a hockey pro, right?"

"He is."

I slide the cup of tea to him before I grab my own. "Close?"

A fond little smile curls on his lips. "Shaw and I are not as close as I would like. The age difference perhaps plays a role, but when we see one another, you wouldn't know it. The messages we exchange when we play his team are hysterical."

"I bet." Leaning against the opposite counter, I get comfortable.

"My mom has never been a great cook, and one year she accidentally burned an elf doll pretending to eat cookies to ashes because the roast chicken on Christmas Day came out on fire from the oven."

My jaw drops because that is hilarious.

"My dad was prepared for a mishap, so had already ordered Chinese food. The eggrolls were pretty damn good that year."

I laugh because he's more upbeat than I thought. "We seem to talk about our family a lot when we run into one another. I guess we are family people."

He snorts a laugh. "Sure. But I am by no means rushing to have my own family. I'm not sure I even have the personality to be a parent. I'll stick to having family photos in my living room."

"Huh, okay. But do you actually have a cozy home? Because I am getting the vibe that you just live out of a suitcase and might only occasionally turn on the washing machine if the dry cleaner is closed."

His cheeks remain light and tight. "This is where I need to tell you that actually I have a house where I can unwind. And even though I will not be handing out candy to little heathens, I have a bowl of Halloween candy in my kitchen purely for aesthetic because it's October."

"No!" I gasp and grin. He nods his confirmation. I raise my hand with stretched fingers into the air. "Mind blown right now."

He bites the inside of his cheek and tilts his head gently to the side, and it's clear he has a sinister thought from my sentence, but it kind of feels natural between us, so I don't think twice. Instead, I switch gears. "I'm kind of surprised to run into you. I assumed you don't really, well..." My lips slide side to side. "Have a life outside of hockey. Then again, you were with a colleague."

He hears the humor in my tone, thankfully. "Sometimes I wonder if I have a non-work life, then I remind myself that I need to shut off, even if just for an hour."

"That's a good mindset. When you are a creative person, you have the problem of never being able to calm your brain. Sometimes I just want to sleep but a design hits me, and I can't help but want to draw."

He takes a quick sip of his tea then indicates with his long finger to the pile of notebooks at the end of my counter. "Are those them?"

"Some." He reaches out, but I tsk. "Invading privacy, huh?" I tease. His eyes tell me that he isn't an easy man to challenge.

"Just dresses?"

"And lingerie. Lots of lingerie," I say bluntly. "It's always lace season," I taunt.

The way he licks his lips and his eyes glue onto me gives me the sign that he isn't disappointed by our unexpected encounter this evening by the slightest.

"You mentioned Halloween candy if I'm good." The way he says it with a straight face, but with inuendo dripping in his sentence causes my stomach to tighten. He has a domineering presence.

But I'm still testing the waters of where this evening might go, if anywhere at all. With purpose, our eyes locked, I walk to the bowl that I have in the corner by the toaster and ceremonially pick it up, returning to him to offer him a piece.

His eyes drop down, and he smiles. "Alright, you have good options. I approve. I was a little worried you might have gummies or those sticks that are pure sugar." He fishes out a chocolate coconut bar, and I swoop up a chocolate caramel bar before setting the bowl down.

"Happy my Halloween candy choices appease you." We both unwrap the candy and pop them into our mouths. "You don't strike me as someone who indulges in candy," I mumble, as I have chocolate in my mouth. Asher is in as good shape as the players on his team.

"Balance. It's about balance, especially when you have a job with grueling days."

I chuckle under my breath. "I'm well aware, and I don't believe it has anything to do with age. If this is where you are highlighting that you're older than me, then you have succeeded. It doesn't matter if we are just two people having a friendly conversation." It's very obvious this is attraction.

"Right." His face says he disagrees, and it's playful in a way.

For a few seconds we stew in the tense air that pulls us closer even without moving.

Suddenly, I remember why we even came up to my apartment.

My eyes drop. "You're lucky your coat protected you. I need to get out of these wet clothes." Maybe there is a tint of sultriness in my tone. "There is more tea over there if you want another cup." He has barely touched his current cup.

Without thought because this is my home, I walk away and begin to peel my sweater up and off my body, then move on to the zipper on my jeans but pause.

The sound of a hum stuck deep in a throat causes me to look back at Asher. His eyes skate over my body then anchors to my eyes.

"You just happen to be wearing that?"

I glance down, and a satisfied smile crawls on my face because I'm in a black lace bra with a touch of orange integrated with the lace of the band. "Yes. Every day I dress in case a fireman needs to save me. I also attempt to coordinate with the holiday."

This wasn't my plan, but I will use this all to my advantage. I'm not someone who is on a mission to come on to him. We are just two people who naturally fall into place around one another, and I might as well enjoy that. I begin to saunter slowly back to him as he begins to loosen the buttons of his shirt around his wrist. His mind is set on something.

A desire.

One that I feel too.

"Lucky me then." His voice is simmering, heavy with determination.

Stopping right in front of him, I ensure our gaze remains tied. "Perhaps so. I still need to take these off." Slowly, I unzip my jeans, ensuring that every tooth pulled is heard.

His breath grows heavy, and his eyes are dark with a dare. Only when I slide down my pants and kick them away does he let his gaze drop, and a muscle in his jaw twitches.

"Careful, little girl, you may have a spirited mouth, but I know how to shut it up."

My skin begins to prickle, and he could touch me between my legs now and be pleased to find me ready for him to take me now if he wanted.

With purpose, I take one step. "You may want to do it then," I challenge.

I plant my fingers on his chest with full intention of unbuttoning his shirt, but he grabs my wrists and holds them up, only to drop his hands, square my hips, and yank me forward. It's a quick move, and I gasp from the surprise, but the rocket of adrenaline shooting up inside of me is welcomed.

"We do it my way. I don't have tolerance for your demands."

My eyes blaze open, and my mouth parts because he *is* what I imagined. "Yes, Coach."

He stands up off the stool as our eyes remained locked. He towers over me, but it suits his dominance that he oozes with every breath.

Our bodies press tighter against one another, and my core tightens below my belly.

"Eager, are we?" he says huskily.

My fingers skim up the buttons of his shirt, still with every intention of unbuttoning every single one. "You have no idea." He allows me to help him be free of his shirt.

The moment it lands on the floor carelessly, he begins to walk me backward with his hands remaining firm on my hips. I feel an urge to beg for him to touch me in other places. His hands are strong; I feel it in the way the pads of his fingers press into my skin.

My body is molten, and he hasn't even kissed me yet. Without direction, he leads us to my bedroom, determined. He kicks the door shut behind him, a hint of his domineering personality that I already assumed he had. The moment that he stills us at the edge of my bed, I feel my heart pounding. I don't need to glance down to see my racing pulse.

Asher must know that my panties are drenched, yet he is prolonging every second on purpose.

"Well, well, well. It seems I have you in a perfect spot to fuck you." It's almost sly the way he says it but also deliciously sexy.

"Is that so? Because you still have too many clothes on," I remind him.

His deep chuckle is sinister, maybe it's a warning, because the moment his breath begins to track down my neck,

I shiver. He's intentionally teasing me, but it is effective, as my body begins to arch against his. The moment his teeth begin to graze my collarbone, a soft croon escapes me.

"You are very patient," he murmurs as his mouth trails back up my neck to my jawline.

"Not going to lie, I'm losing it," I comment with a breathy voice.

That's when my world tilts in a different way because his lips finally meet mine. There is no chance for soft or gentle. He claims my mouth in an overpowering kiss while his hands travel up my body to frame my face and keep me trapped and balanced. His mouth slants, and my tongue seeks entrance to meet his, and he grants it. The tip of his tongue plays with mine, a tickle. His lips are firm and full, and I get a millisecond of air before he presses his lips back onto mine. This time, I kiss back with more insistence that the kiss is deep. He gives me that for a breath before the feeling of our kiss softening brings tingles between my legs. The kiss is sensual and only makes me want more.

But in one swift move, he pushes me down onto the mattress, and I bite the corner of my lower lip while I smirk. Tutting, I wave a finger side to side at him. "Tsk, tsk, you still have pants on."

A chuckle rumbles deep in his throat right before the click of his belt fills the room.

"I'm not liking your bratty mouth," he reprimands.

I fake a pout. "Oh, silly me, I forgot to obey, Coach."

Asher steps out of his pants, and with speed, he leans down to harshly drag my panties down my legs, our eyes never breaking contact. "Open your legs," he demands.

Gladly, I obey, well aware though not shy about the fact that I'm wet.

His head inches back, inspecting, and his mouth slowly

curls into a half smirk filled with satisfaction. "Look at that. Someone wants my cock."

My eyes hood closed, and I'm speechless until I gasp at the feeling of two fingers swiping along my pussy, circling my clit, and it's a heavenly torture.

"You're soaking," he whispers.

"Mmhmm."

His fingers stay on me, but with his other hand, he roughly pulls down one cup of my bra, to give him the open canvas to twist my nipple. But it doesn't last long because my pussy is pulsing for more.

"You're beautiful."

I can't even acknowledge the compliment because my entire body is heightened with arousal and at his mercy.

His fingers abandon my clit and glide along my thigh, giving me hope that he will end this agony of waiting to come.

The loss of his touch causes my eyes to flick open, but my thoughts are rewarded because my view is Asher with his large cock in his hand, giving himself a few pumps. He quickly opens the condom packet and sheathes himself.

The moment he hovers over me, placing a quick kiss on my mouth, a new frequency of adrenaline hits me all over again.

My breath hitches because his cock slides into me, and I instantly feel full. Slowly, he moves until I'm filled to the hilt.

"Fuck. You are..."

I plant my finger over his mouth. "Shh. Just fuck me," I gasp.

That devilish smirk returns to his mouth, and he rises slightly to his knees as he guides my legs to wrap around his waist, and my internal walls wrap even tighter around his length.

He pumps into me, not treating me delicately, but his groan meets my moan which assures me that we are riding the same wave.

It's a blissful blur until he pushes his finger on my clit while he slams into me, causing an orgasm. I convulse all over him, and he follows moments later, an almost roar escaping his lips.

And it makes sense because he fucks like an animal, but every little second is perfectly bossy, and it suits him.

I sigh blissfully, thankful that Illinois's unpredictable October weather gave me this.

# CHAPTER 4
## ASHER

I can't help but look at Gracie peculiarly. Does she ever frown? We are lying on our sides facing one another after round two, because we might as well take advantage of our detour for the night. The sheet is carelessly covering her breasts.

She tries to keep her face stern, but it is a failure because she bursts out in a laugh. "Seriously, I'm sorry, but seeing you smile kind of unnerves me. It's not some sexy ploy, instead it's an honest, normal smile."

I playfully shove her shoulder. "I do smile. Of course, I do. I have media to deal with. Wins to celebrate."

We've been talking for who knows how long. Pillow talk normally isn't my style, except she causes me to crack from my usual scowl.

"Now, now, we've gone over this, Mr. Coach. That's all work. I don't know, it kind of alarms me but makes me laugh the way you look after sex. It's like endorphins or something."

Shrugging my shoulder, I have to admit that I feel lighter right now. "You're kind of contagious. Do you ever have a bad day? You seem overly positive with life." I swipe a strand of her hair over her arm.

"I don't look at it that way. I've been fortunate, and I don't take that for granted. Family, work, small-town antics. A state-prized cow lives on the edge of town, that's great, isn't it?" Now she is just being sarcastic, but it earns a chuckle from me.

"I'll admit small-town life is refreshing."

"Have you tried the orange rolls from Jolly Joe's in Lake Spark? You need to, otherwise you haven't lived life."

My brows shoot up. "Oh yeah? Looks like I live a boring life then."

She quiets and seems to be thinking over something as her bright demeanor begins to fade. "Maybe I've been living in a protected shell. That might not be a good thing. Life can't always be a party, right? I'm sure life will throw something at me to remind me that not everything is easy."

I lie back until I'm staring at the ceiling with my arms tucked behind my head. "Don't wish for it. Some people go through life like a breeze."

She blows out a breath, causing the hair near her hairline to flip to the side. "Still. Even people who breeze on by have their tough moments. Maybe I feel as though a crack will hit my life somewhere. Isn't there something that happened that has bothered you your whole life? Something that sticks in your head that you don't quite understand?"

I take a few ticks to think about it, but then a first happens for me; I feel words easily flow out of my mouth. "I guess that I always felt the need to impress my parents and people. It makes zero sense because my parents are the type to be proud of anything I do. My little brother always looked up to me. It's my own drive to perfection."

"That happens. For me, my mom kind of always incorporated me into her life on an equal level. Most assume that I'm following in her shoes because that's what is expected or it's an easy handout for me. I don't see it that way. We have different design styles, and it's a tradition that I want to follow. Other people can go screw themselves… although I still don't like it if they have that view of me."

"I get that."

"Any skeletons in your closet? There must be a crazy ex or maybe a fiancée that didn't work out." She thrums her fingers on the mattress, eager for the gossip.

"Nah, nothing earth shattering. I'm just a tense ball, remember. My last girlfriend was a model I didn't date for long. Dinner conversations got boring." Her lips roll in as if she's fighting a retort. I raise a brow at her. "Yes? Care to share with the room?"

She shrugs. "Nothing. It's just a little cliché, that's all. My last Prince not-so-Charming just became a dreaded ball of negativity. He was not pleased about my family's holiday enthusiasm, and I have zero tolerance for someone who makes me choose between being close with family and them."

"*Yeah.* Good thing you ditched him… and why are we talking about our dating life while naked in bed after sex?"

She swats me playfully. "Well, I don't think you exactly want to go over the photos I saw online of you at the team holiday party. There were eggplant emojis in the comments. In case you would like the 411."

I cringe at everything in that sentence. "Don't remind me of the hour from hell. I fear Christmas. If the marketing team brings out fucking reindeer antlers, then I'm going to consider storing a flask in my front suit pocket."

Her sexy little finger pokes my shoulder as she begins to shuffle. I turn my head to catch her finger between my teeth for a bite. "Oh dear, it seems you have trauma that needs to be tended to." She flashes her eyes at me, and in a swift move, straddles me.

But I won't be having her lead the way. I'm quick to flip her to her back and hold her wrists above her head against the mattress while her hips lifting to mine is agony. She's trying to entice me, and in a few hours, I will leave. She is apparently the escape I haven't had in a while or perhaps at all. There have always been expectations with others. Now? I get to relax, turn off my thoughts of hockey, and have physical gratification in the process. I would like to have a morning session, but that won't be happening.

With a heavy sigh, I let her go and roll to the side to sit up on the edge of the mattress, searching for my boxer briefs. I feel a need to pop our bubble because something unsettles me, this gravitating pull to this woman that has my thoughts wrapped in a knot. "I won't be here when you get up."

She chokes on a laugh. "Really? Wouldn't have guessed." Her humor is a relief.

I glance over my shoulder to give her a knowing look. It's a struggle to pinpoint what it is about her that is a thrilling unease. My mind strikes clarity. "I have a career to tend to, and besides…"

Her hand gently touches my back. "This is what this is. A little release. We both know the score."

"Exactly." I stand to pull up my boxer briefs. "Want some water?"

Looking back at her sitting up and holding the sheet up to her breasts has me second-guessing my restraint level to actually leave later.

There is a reckless voice inside me that is whispering, but I shove it to the side.

"That would be great. I need to freshen up anyhow."

I nod and leave her be. I make myself at home in her kitchen and grab two waters from the fridge and sigh because I'm freaking tired. The weather is a good excuse because there is no way that I'll make the drive back now anyhow. I'll take a quick shower here, then be at the rink by six. I always have an extra set of clothes in my car.

Returning to the bedroom, I stall and stare up at the ceiling as I groan, before scraping my free hand across my face. "Are you kidding me?" I can't help but smile ear to ear.

"What?" Gracie plays dumb as she sits in the middle of her bed in black satin shorts that show off her legs and a tank. "I always go to bed like this." I gawk at her, not convinced. Tossing the bottles of water to the other side of the mattress, I crawl onto her bed. Her honest laugh is easy on the ears. "Seriously. Hello? Reminder of what I do for a living. And even if I go with the cotton collection, it's cute."

The temptation is refueling again. "So tonight, you couldn't go for the cotton."

"Well, no. You dress to match the appropriate event."

She's a temptress, and I bet when she looks into my eyes, she sees my wicked plans. "At least you're honest. But this isn't good for us. I feel like you might get frisky at two in the morning."

She juts her leg out and presses her pointed toe against my chest to keep me at bay. "You might, and I'm already at your service with easy access," she taunts in her voice that is pure sex and sin.

"Smart decision then. Come on, I need at least an hour of sleep before I fuck you senseless again."

"Getting old, are you?"

Instantly, I grab her thigh and pull her to her side and spank her ass. "Don't be naughty, otherwise I will tie you up."

"Do it," she rasps.

Of course, she would say that.

"I will just take a little rest. Your pussy needs it too."

"Considerate of you."

We both settle under the covers, and I'm not sure if it's the silence or the orgasms that I had, but we both manage to drift off to sleep.

Only to wake a few hours later, and without any words, I slid right into her. Spooning from behind, I took her slow until the very last minute when I went in deep and hard, our bodies tight together as her tits jiggled with every pump and moan. We both seemed to sync our orgasm before falling into a sated slumber.

I've never considered myself a cuddler. Hell, I never spend nights with women. It's a quick gratification kind of thing. But with Gracie? I'm breaking a few rules. I know because of the bedside clock and the fact there is warmth from her sleeping body pressed against mine, with my arm wrapped around her. As if it's all some natural instinct.

Somewhere just before five, I sneak out of bed to leave. Dressing, I make it to the door of her bedroom and pause to glance over my shoulder to take a mental picture of Gracie stirring in bed.

"It was fun. Good luck with the game," she mumbles groggily.

My jaw ticks because I'm not sure if I should half smile from that comment. She's making this too easy.

"Sleep. You deserve it," I whisper.

And she deserves more than a night too. But she seemed to be on board with whatever silent one-night arrangement we had, and I can walk away with one night. A perfect release, a perfect fit to my body, and now I can focus on my almost perfect career.

# CHAPTER 5
## ASHER

## 4 WEEKS LATER

Not going to lie. I'm dragging my feet and pasting on a smile as I sip on my wine. Red wine wouldn't be my choice for Thanksgiving Day because it's heavy paired with the dinner buffet and my physical state. But when the team owner invites you to stop by on Thanksgiving Day, you don't say no. Especially since he knows that I didn't have particular plans. We got back extremely late last night from our away game, and I can count the number of hours that I slept on one hand.

Declan smiles at me as we stand in the living room near the floor-to-ceiling window overlooking the lake. "Thanks for stopping by. Violet wouldn't be impressed if you didn't show. She has a thing for inviting everyone and then worries if she missed someone who doesn't have any plans."

"The thought of driving up to Chicago for the day only to turn back around wasn't exactly my idea of holiday fun, so I'm happy to be here," I reply. My parents were understanding of the plan, anyhow.

He looks down into his drink. "Still, last year when she found out the rookie from Germany had no place to go, she cried for a solid ten minutes until my nephew, Connor, assured her that he was with him." None of us asks about the dynamics between Declan and our team captain who happens to be his nephew. For most people, it would be considered nepotism, but everyone in the organization sees it purely as talent deserved. I'm familiar with the dynamic with my own family.

The house is crowded, which makes me wonder how his wife would even notice if a rookie was missing, but some people are just great hosts like that. Apparently, the last coach was an anti-social asshole which is why it was a welcome relief to the team when I managed to laugh during first practice.

Noticing Hudson Arrows in the corner talking with someone as they both balance a piece of pie on a plate, it causes me to wonder. "Is there anybody from the hockey world or Lake Spark that isn't here?"

Declan glances over his shoulder to eye the scene that I'm looking at. "Today, there is no hockey talk. Hudson is actually neighbors with my brother-in-law. Their kids grew up together."

*Huh.*

That means Gracie.

I haven't seen her around, but it doesn't mean that she hasn't floated into my mind uninvited. Instead, I have flashes of her on top of me and under me, depending on my mood. Most definitely she is responsible for my hand when I'm in the shower, and she has no idea.

Sometimes, I think about contacting her for one more time. We both need an escape, right? What's the harm in another night or even a few spare hours?

"I need to check on my wife. Happy wife means a happy life. You should grab a piece of the pecan pie, it's a recipe that uses my family's maple syrup farm." He winks at me.

"I think I will be in trouble if I tell you that the pumpkin pie is calling my name."

He grins then walks away, and I mosey to the dessert table in the corner. The options are endless, but the pecan pie actually takes the win.

"You can eat it but be prepared for the shot of bourbon inside because someone got excited about it when baking," Connor, my team captain, warns me as he grabs a small plate. He mentioned the other day on the plane that he, his wife, and their twins always spend it with his family.

"Thanks for the heads-up. Might be good to really wake me up."

He blows out a breath. "Tell me about it. Getting back late then having the twins eager to start the day at six is a little brutal."

Sometimes I think about the whole wife-and-family life. It's not that it isn't appealing, it's just that I have no space or time in my life for it. The players have games and practice, maybe a few endorsement deals. A coach? We have games, practice, watching videos, team meetings, general manager meetings, and the list goes on.

Using the pie cutter, I attempt to pull off a piece of the pie but stop mid-slice when I notice Gracie walk into the room.

Throw ice on me.

The pine-green turtleneck sweater she's wearing covers up fuck all in my mind. I still envision every curve underneath or the way her tongue licks my skin. Also, I wasn't expecting her here, and my body needs a minute to adjust.

She spots me by accident, and her eyes blaze in slight recognition.

"Okay, a slice of apple and that's it. There is fruit somewhere in this thing, and I don't need the girls hyped up on more sugar," I hear Connor say, and in the corner of my eye, he walks away.

Gracie takes a deep breath and quickly searches the room to see if anyone has noticed her. Slowly, she ambles my way to land right in front of the table. She doesn't look at me when she arrives, instead taking an unsteady breath and pretending to study the options.

"Hi," she says faintly.

"Hi." I give up on the pie and turn to face her, even if our eyes don't meet. "I wasn't expecting to see you here."

"We always stop by on Thanksgiving. All of my dad's friends are here, actually." She glances over her shoulder as if to check that nobody is watching.

A heavy pause lingers in the air. Small talk is probably the way to go. "Want a piece of pie? I hear there is an overload of alcohol in the pecan."

I notice the way her body stiffens, and she seems to swallow as if she needs to balance herself. "Oh gosh no, the mere thought of pie in any shape or form makes me want to gag."

Creases appear on my forehead. "Why?

She blows out a breath. "Because the plate of food that I nibbled on in the kitchen tasted rancid."

"Really? I thought all of the food here was pretty good. Gourmet, even."

She presses her fingertips against her lips. "Was it? Maybe it's my tastebuds or something. I've been fighting a stomach virus all week. Half of the people coming into the boutique are sick and spreading germs." Finally, she lifts her gaze and shifts her shoulder, meaning her body is angled to me for our eyes to meet.

It's electric. Instantly, we are tied together purely by our sight.

Gracie is still gorgeous, but I would be lying if I said I could ignore the dark circles under her eyes that she attempted to cover up. "Tired too?"

The line of her pressed lips stretches a tad. "Totally. What gave it away? I must look like a zombie."

"I know the feeling. Whoever from the league planned our team schedule should be given a penalty."

She chuckles under her breath. "At least, you've had a few good games."

I'm slightly surprised and impressed. "You've been watching again?"

She shrugs one shoulder, and her smile is nuanced. "Hockey can be interesting. Besides, there is this new coach that I hear is an ass, but he looks good in a suit, so…"

Licking my lips, I enjoy her saying that. "Lucky him."

Her lips roll in and cheeks tighten because she seems entertained. "He was once."

There is the reminder of the night we spent together. Our eyes recognize our mutual thoughts, and the brief silence is needed.

"That he was," I mention in barely a whisper.

The corner of her mouth twitches from my statement before she visibly shakes her thoughts away. "Anyhow, here we are. It was bound to happen, and better now than the upcoming holiday parties, with dancing elves and sitting on Santa's lap. Something tells me that I'm going on the naughty list." Her flirty tone is bold considering where we are.

Taking a tiny step closer, I feel the current between us, but I don't particularly want to speak a smidgen louder. "If you're on the naughty list, then I'm on the going-to-the-gates-of-Hell list."

She snorts a laugh. "On that day, you can be on the side of the family who don't believe in hell," she teases me.

"Oh yeah, I can play that card."

She takes a deep breath. "I'm not sure what we are supposed to say since we kind of left things pretty clear."

"We're just making small talk, aren't we?"

Her brows lift then fall before she sighs. "Yeah. In front of the dessert table that smells like a sugar overload."

"Damn, you really hate every attempt at very edible food in this place." I can't seem to tear my eyes away from her. I'm pulled in, intrigued, and simply enjoy the social interaction. That's what people do at these things, and maybe we are lucky and nobody notices the way we interact with one another.

Gracie pinches the bridge of her nose. "Sorry. I'm just tired and not feeling like this is the place to be right now. Bed is a lot more appealing." That grabs my interest, and maybe the half smirk I have shows it. "Probably not the thing to say to you." Her nervous smile is honest, and I notice her blush.

"Sensible," I comment blandly.

Her head lolls to the side, and her smile remains but is now a little more relaxed. "Uhm, I would invite you over but sleep really is in my calling, and so be it that I sleep in next to nothing." Her low voice that only I can hear is a crime because we are in public.

"You're trouble again, aren't you?"

She shrugs. "Depends what your mind is thinking."

My lips quirk out as I gather my composure, as she is a little temptress, and I didn't realize how much she's been in my head. Until now when she is standing in front of me with a peculiar sparkle in her eyes and her entire existence from body to words has me wanting a little more of her.

Reminding myself where I am, I step back and scan the

room. It's a party, and everyone is in their own conversations, but the world seems small around us.

My guess is that Gracie notices how I've undressed her with my eyes a few times now, and she knows because she's done the same. However, we are smart people.

"I have to get up early, so I'm going to head out," I explain seriously. No inuendo at all.

Her lips pop. "And I need to just take it easy tonight. Tomorrow is our Black Friday sale, so the boutique and online store will go insane."

We both just stand there, neither one of us making an effort to part.

Except, she does it again. Her chest rises and her face stills as she struggles to open her mouth and instead visibly swallows. She's a little gray, and it's clear that a room full of people is the last place she should be.

"Are you sure you're okay?"

"Totally," she lies. "It's just the smell of apple pie or something. I'm just not in the mood to eat lately. It's been crunch time for work, so my body is everywhere."

Holidays are a stressful period. I hate it, and then add on the hockey schedule and I'm surprised I have any moments to stop and have a normal night of sleep.

"Okay."

She offers me a soft smile and swipes her hair to one shoulder. Her beauty is classic, without all the effort many women her age tend to do with makeup. I want to touch her, but the moment I step close, I stop myself and clear my throat, straightening my posture. I'm wiser than that.

"Take care. Maybe the universe won't make us wait another month before we see one another again," she quips.

"Maybe," I answer faintly as our shoulders brush in the process of her walking past me.

I turn my head slightly to watch her go in my peripheral view. I'm entranced. She gives me this peculiar feeling which forms a pit in my stomach.

She says goodbye to her dad and mom across the room, and I notice the way her mom feels Gracie's forehead as if she is a child, and it causes her to step back, humorously annoyed, then she leaves.

Hopefully, she feels better.

Sighing a deep breath, I decide that I'm not in the mood for dessert, even though my eyes are now fixed on the pies. Maybe it's more to give me something to look at while I cool my thoughts.

Has it really been almost a month since I saw her?

It sticks in my mind and not because I'm pining for her. No, it sticks in my mind for a reason I can't figure out.

It feels reckless.

Then it clicks.

Gracie isn't feeling well, and it's been a month. I'm confident we were careful—wait, maybe that part is a little hazy. Well, actually, we might've been lax somewhere on the birth control front during our many rounds.

Shit. Is she? No. Nope. She's not feeling well, and it's been a month.

There is only one thought in my mind, and it fills me with a rage that I didn't know possible. It's not even from fury, only fear.

I'm not going to wait. Whether she's already aware or not, I want an answer if she is pregnant today.

# CHAPTER 6
## GRACIE

Who the hell decided cranberry sauce goes well with stuffing? I mean, sure, every year until this one it's been a great combo, but this year someone really must have gone off the recipe card. Maybe the can of sauce was out of date. I don't know, but my stomach is not happy.

Looking in the mirror of my bathroom, my dark blue cotton pajama jumpsuit with snowflakes on it seems to complement the gray tint on my face, and I look as though I haven't slept for days, which makes zero sense, as all I've been is tired. I even managed to throw in a nap yesterday after taking the holiday decorations out of my closet. But I'm just waiting for my period. It can be wacky on dates sometimes.

Opening the door to my bedroom, I yelp in fright, my hand going straight to my chest. My heart is racing, shocked to find Asher sitting on the edge of my bed.

"What the hell?" I lean over with my hand on my chest to settle my nerves.

Although I'm relieved it's only him, I don't quite understand how he got into my home or why he has a hardened look and his icy eyes are spearing into me. He's in a suit which tells me that he must have come straight from the party. If his mood wasn't so disconcerting, then I would drink in the sight of him a little more. He has the ability to mesmerize me into a trance.

"How did you get in here?"

He glances to his side on the mattress before driving his gaze straight back at me. "Take the test." He's direct and stern. His whole demeanor makes me want to slap him as much as kiss him. He's bossy and sexy and… my eyes drift to the mattress where he seems to have brought a pile of pregnancy tests.

"Excuse me?" I blink a few times, half-pissed off at his authoritarian attitude and angry because he, well… won't let me not confront what might have slipped into my mind a time or two the last few days.

"Take the test," he repeats, this time gritting out the words.

I rest my hand against the door frame to my bathroom, forgetting that my pajamas barely make it halfway down my thighs but his eyes appraising me for a few seconds remind me.

"You have some audacity to storm on in here, which how the hell did you? And then demand that I take a pregnancy test." I'm a bit offended—or I'm just buying myself time.

Asher taps a long finger on one of the test boxes. "Don't leave your key under the pot no matter if the town's biggest worry is a wild deer. And take the damn test."

"It was a goat gone rogue," I correct him.

He contritely lifts the edges of his mouth into a closed smile. "Test. Now."

My jaw lowers, and my mouth goes dry. My voice seems to be lost.

His face remains icy. "I'm not blind. I noticed how you nearly threw up at the buffet a few times. Or the fact that your sass was a little less tonight. No matter how beautiful you are, it can't be denied that you look like you have sea sickness, even though we are on fucking land. Then, funny thing, I'm great with numbers." Inhaling a sharp breath, I listen to him. "Need those numbers for penalty kills and power play percentages, and I also need numbers when looking at a calendar and counting back. So, take the fucking test, maybe three while we are at it," he bites out.

My lips roll in as I accept his facts, and my breath picked up already when he mentioned throwing up. I scoff a sound and propel my body away from the bathroom to the chair in the corner that has a robe that matches my pajamas, and I slide it on and tie the belt. "Don't be ridiculous. There are flus going around."

*Don't make me take a test. Please.*

His eyes go wide at my statement. "You don't believe that, nor do I. Leave the robe off and please take a test."

Angerly, I throw my robe off. *Hot instruction.* My hands land on my hips. "You really have some audacity coming in here."

A shade a sympathy floods his face as he stands and saunters to me. "Look, I'm sure you're scared, but you can't lie to me right now. Could you be pregnant?"

My mouth opens and words get stuck halfway up my throat, then I smile nervously. "Don't be ridiculous... Okay, yes, fine. There could be a chance." I give up.

He catches my chin with his forefinger and thumb to guide my eyes to meet his. "Denial, huh." His voice has softened.

I attempt to look away, but he almost affectionately draws my sight back to him. "Maybe something like that."

"Time to confront it, don't you think?"

Breaking away from his fingers, I sigh. "You're right," I admit.

"We need to know."

The way he says *we* pokes me gently inside. I barely nod, and he steps back to the pile of tests, picks one up, and breaks the wrapping.

Walking to him, I peer over his shoulder. "Was there a sale or something?" It's *almost* funny. There are like eight tests.

He shrugs. "You never know how many we'll need." He nearly shoves the test in my hand.

Inhaling a deep breath, I accept this situation then disappear into the bathroom. When I emerge again, Asher is sitting exactly where he was the last time I crossed this doorway. This time, his body is more subdued and his fingers thrum along the edge of the mattress.

"And?" His eyes widen.

I hold up the stick. "We wait a few minutes."

I sit next to him, and he scooches over to make space. Sitting side by side, I feel his warmth and inhale the scent of his cologne; today it reminds me of cardamom. Our vision drills into the test stick that is face down in my hand. The silence is unbearable, and I can hear an invisible ticking clock in my head. We sit there for a few minutes until I accept that the time is up.

A breath escapes my pursed lips, and I slowly flip the stick.

*And my world just changed forever.*

"Shit," Asher grits out, and he rubs his face, his mouth

gaped open. My stomach does a giant somersault. "Take another test."

I hop up to standing. "Screw that. Give me all of them." I hold out my hands, and I'm determined to prove this test wrong. Thank goodness I didn't empty my bladder because of the whisper in the back of my head that maybe I would need to take another test.

He's in full agreement and scoops up the boxes and gives them to me. I'm quick to disappear into the bathroom, and five minutes later, we both look down in astonishment at the row of tests on my bathroom counter.

Two lines. Red circle. Two lines again. Oh look, a digital one that says pregnant, in case my mind still needs clarification.

"*So…*" I say as we both stare blankly at our fate.

"I guess I should be thankful on this Thanksgiving Day that there was a store open so I could spend my evening staring at tests that confirm that you are indeed pregnant." His quip falls flat, but he gets a point for attempting to joke.

"It's yours, in case you were wondering." I can't drag my eyes away, and I take a deep breath because I'm dizzy from this news. "I'm not some puck bunny who planned to seduce you then trap you—"

He holds his hand up to stop me. "I wasn't thinking that. You have no reason to trap me. And you didn't exactly seduce me. You are just far too sexually confident that I find you intoxicating. A firecracker that makes me thoughtless on the birth control front."

"Are you saying this is my fault?"

"No. I'm saying you are a woman with power who casts spells on people."

I blink a few times. "So, I'm Frau Perchta?"

His eyes widen at me, and he gooses his neck. "Who the fuck is Frau Perchta?"

"The German witch of winter. Some say she is actually a goddess. She can reward or punish you, especially during the twelve days of Christmas, and it's now winter."

He shakes his head side to side, and his finger indicates to wrap it up. "We're going off track, but we will go with the goddess part. And we are both responsible for our birth control fail. Which everything else except procreation I'm good on when it comes to the eighth-grade safe sex talk, that I clearly once ignored as a grown man."

"Me too."

"Now let's talk about this baby. You. Me. A baby, to be exact."

I'm slightly relieved by his compliment, even if it wasn't meant to be one. Silence lingers in my bathroom again as my new reality sinks in. Finally, he touches my arm, and we both drag our eyes away from the view of our confirmation.

"We should probably talk." His sincerity is strong.

Before I can respond, an overpowering lightheadedness sweeps through me, and my body becomes the Leaning Tower of Pisa. Asher is quick to offer me support, and his hand takes a grip on my arm.

"Come on, you should lie down on your side," he insists and helps guide me to my bed.

"It's the news. My body is just trying to deal with the shock… Okay, it's probably a pregnancy symptom, like all the other ones I've been in denial about." My voice is faint, and my eyes feel heavy as Asher aids me to lie on my side.

He tosses the throw blanket on me that I keep on the edge of my bed and leans down. "Just rest."

Swallowing, I'm not sure what to say or ask. Only the obvious. "What now?"

His sigh is strong and fills the room while our eyes link for a few beats before he stands and begins to pace the floor. Rubbing his temples, he is thinking. "I don't know." He seems frustrated. "I have to be on a flight first thing in the morning to Philly. I can't think right now."

Attempting to sit up, I fall right back down. "We should take a breather. Discuss this in a few days."

"We have options." He stops mid-pace, and his sentence slices through me, and maybe he senses that. "Just… you're right… take a few days and let the news sink in."

Is his body language already indicating what he wants? Is his mind already made up? What do I want?

"Okay, we're on the same page about waiting to discuss. When are you back?"

"Sunday."

I focus on taking a few breaths, accepting that the next few days won't be easy. "Then we'll talk then."

The sting in the corner of my eye and the strain in my throat begins, indicating tears are about to break out.

"Are you mad?" I wonder.

Asher rubs his face and chuckles bitterly under his breath. "This definitely wasn't the surprise that I was planning on."

So, he *is* angry.

"Neither was I."

He shakes his head. "My focus should be on one thing: the team. This is my time to make my mark and turn the organization around. Distractions are the last thing I need, but here we are." He sounds annoyed.

I'm beginning to get pissed off, and I sit up, dizziness be damned. "Yeah, here we are," I volley back, completely deflated.

"Gracie, we can both admit that neither one of us had this in our future planning right now."

I bite my lip tucked into my mouth and try to fight the stream of tears that fills me because an overwhelming feeling comes over me not to be disappointed with this news.

He watches me and maybe he realizes that he is being insensitive or lacking tact in his choice of words. "Just… let's take a breather and give ourselves a few days," he reaffirms. Rubbing the back of his neck, he blows out another breath. "You'll be alright now? I mean, you don't seem to be feeling well." At least his concern is convincing.

Shrugging, I feel the need to state the obvious that we've now figured out. "I'm pregnant, remember? This comes with the territory."

He slowly nods, and his cheeks tighten from the reality. "Right. Pregnant," he repeats to himself. Throwing his thumb over his shoulder, he has a pained expression. "I should go then, if you don't need anything right now. You need rest."

"Yeah, sure. Don't let the door hit you on the way out." I'm kind of pissed off, and I'm not exactly sure the root of it. Asher has every right to deal with his shock in his own way. Maybe I'm just too sensitive. Hormones, right?

He gawks at me from my brazen attitude. "Sunday. I'll see you Sunday."

I bob my head groggily and let my head fall onto my pillow as he sees himself out.

Staring up at the ceiling, I accept that I'm completely lost right now.

# CHAPTER 7
## ASHER

That was a brutal loss. I mean, we still got a point for the standings because we went into overtime, but I hate the coach from the other team. He wastes all of our time calling out to the referee for every single damn push on the ice and then complains in press conferences about the tactics of my defensemen. My cold reception to our guys in the locker room after the game probably wasn't warranted, but I had aggression to get out, and it had nothing to do with them, unfortunately. Maybe it was my own personal meltdown. But my demeanor softened for a second when our goalie showed his phone to the team, with the screen filled with photos of his seven-month-old and his face covered with sweet potato while he wore a ridiculous little turkey hat.

Needless to say, I went quiet, and maybe it was too eerie for the team, because Tyler broke my daze and asked if I was okay. I'm entering the same daze again as I sit on a bench on Main Street in Everhope. The windows decorated in holiday decorations are in an odd way calming. The little boy crossing the street holding his mom's hand while she carries shopping bags in the other reminds me of why I'm sitting here with a coffee in hand and waiting for Gracie.

I'm well aware that I will not be receiving any awards for my reaction the other day. I've thought about this on so many levels. I'm a man of strong integrity and character. I'm going to take responsibility, whatever Gracie chooses.

But a baby isn't a career. It's a whole new realm that I'm not familiar with. I also can't be the guy who gives money and stands at a distance, seeing their child once a year. I'm probably not the typical candidate for father of the year, but in hockey and in life, there is always a wild card thrown at you. Maybe I could even become father of the year. If I'm as determined to do well with that role as I am being a coach, then I could put the same effort into being a damn good dad. However, for once, I'm not a pro at something. I'm back to being a rookie, except I *really* can't fuck up this game because it isn't one at all; it's a baby.

It's nerve-wracking as hell, but it keeps repeating in my head what to do. A shiver runs through me, because despite the lack of snow, Illinois is still freezing this time of year.

Taking a sip of my coffee, my eyes flick up when I see Gracie approaching, and my heartrate speeds up because here we are a few days later to talk. She slows her arrival and tightens her maroon-colored scarf around her neck over her gray coat.

"Is this seat taken?" Her smile is weak, and she must be nervous too.

I scoot over to make room. "No, it was waiting for you."

She sits down, and we both look forward and sit in silence. How the hell do we begin this conversation?

"Foxy Rox put a train in the window among fake snow," I comment, and I guess that's how we are starting.

"I noticed." She begins to make a noise. "Speaking of

coffee, is that coffee that you are drinking?" She visibly swallows then covers her mouth.

"Yes." My face contorts because I'm a little lost.

She presses her fingers against her lips. "Yeah, the smell makes me want to vomit."

*Huh... oh, wait.*

"Noted." I stand and quickly jog to discard the drink in the trash can by the newspaper box on the corner that nobody uses anymore, then return to Gracie. "Morning sickness?"

She tilts her head to the side. "Something like that." Her sight remains razored to the ground.

I guess this is a good entry point into the serious conversation that we need to have. "Look, Grac—"

"I'm keeping the baby." She blurts out her interruption then turns her head to face me, her eyes heavy, but there is a glint of delicate tenacity. Maybe she wants to see my reaction.

The breath that I take feels heavy but right. "We're doing this."

"Is that what you want?" She sounds a little doubtful.

I nod subtly. "Yeah. I'm in this."

It's obvious that her body is flooding with relief. "Okay… Not going to lie, I was hoping you would say that. I've been freaking out for a few days now."

I can't help but chuff a laugh. "*Yeah*, freaking out might be an understatement." We both share that.

A small smile begins to creep onto her face that has radiance that was missing the other day. "I've been walking around a lot to think. Did you know the park has reindeer right now? I'm not sure they are really happy since they are in a kind of pen, but an elf feeds them hay and kids watch." I grimace at her because she's rambling, and she shakes her head when she realizes. "Anyhow, on my walks I just kept thinking only one thing… I want this. Completely not planned, but no other thought has entered my brain."

Placing my hand on her thigh to help assure her, I feel the side of my mouth stretch. "I can relate. I needed to adjust to the news. Becoming a dad most definitely was not on my bingo card for the year—or two or five. *But* apparently, the universe wants this to happen now."

"I haven't told anyone."

"Me neither. I'm not exactly sure what happens now."

She shrugs. "Neither do I, but maybe we'll wait to tell anyone. It's early, and everyone is occupied with the holidays anyhow."

"Agreed. Don't you need to see a doctor?"

She adjusts her scarf again. "Not yet. Those tests are very accurate these days, especially when you take eight. I'll call the doctor's office tomorrow."

"Okay. Good… good, good." I grow quiet, and my fingers thrum on her leg. She touches my wrist, and the tiny smirk on her face is because she's maybe amused by me.

"We can figure out other things as we go. We have time. I mean, biology says probably thirty-four weeks, but…" She throws her arms in the air. "Who's counting?"

"The baby is your belly probably is," I reply dryly.

We both seem to be relaxing. We're attempting humor, and that's a start.

I shift on the bench and blow out a whistle. "Your dad is going to kill me."

"He might." Her face turns serious before then she bursts out laughing. "Your parents? What will they think?"

Scratching the back of my head, I think about it for a second. It hasn't crossed my mind since I'm an adult. Lucky for me they are them, warm and always accepting. "Surprised but pretty relaxed. Ignore my mom if she asks if she can take photos during labor, she sometimes forgets boundaries."

Her forehead creases. "As in *during* labor?"

"She's a photographer and loves finding new subjects."

She laughs, and it's good to see a glow returning to her face. "Duly noted. My mom will probably be thrilled. She was pregnant with me before they got married. Actually, my dad arranged a judge to marry them the following week and didn't tell my mom."

My eyes bug out. "Whoa, ballsy..." And traditional. Which kind of brings on the other thought that has been dancing in my head... Gracie and I. "Speaking of which, uh..." There is strain in my voice.

Her hand rushes to touch my arm to calm me. "Oh my God, I didn't bring that up because I think we should... you know... No. We don't need to... Blah, I am not sure what I'm saying, but you don't need to marry me or something like that. We don't know one another that well."

A flood of relief escapes. "Phew, I was a little worried there."

She smiles wryly. "We'll have to get to know one another, I'm the mom and you're the dad."

"That is how biology works, yes." I extend my hand, offering a handshake. Her eyes squinch at my gesture, but then it vanishes when she takes my hand. Her touch gives me an instant zing. "Hi, I'm Asher Tate, the father of your child."

She doesn't let my hand go and grants me an easy smile. "Hi, I'm Gracie Arrows, the mother of your child."

Our eyes are tied just like a ribbon on a Christmas present. Maybe one day I'll figure out if Gracie is the present that my life needed.

Stopping myself from thinking further, I release her hand and feel the absence immediately. Still, I manage to snicker a laugh. "Oh man, this is going to be an adventure, isn't it?" This woman gets me to smile more times than I can count for a conversation that is probably the most serious one of my life.

She sinks back and rests against the bench. "I guess it is."

"I'm sorry if I'm not around as much as I would like. We are about to head into mid-season. I'm not sure how to balance this."

Her mouth slides side to side. "Players and coaches have done it before. So can you. I'm also aware that your schedule in all honesty is shit. But I'm not new to it. My dad was a coach when I was a kid."

I chuckle under my breath. "No more mention of your dad because it freaks me out."

"I shouldn't tell you that he has access to farm tools because my brother works at the Blisswood Winery." She's messing with me again and taking pleasure in that.

"Small world. My parents used to go there all the time for their romantic weekend getaways. It was perfect for me because I was able to throw some epic parties when I was in high school."

She sputters a laugh. "Crossing my fingers that this kid isn't a troublemaker."

"He or she will, of course, be in skates as soon as they can walk."

Her smile doesn't wilt in the slightest. "I could be on board with that."

Our vision connects, and a quiet overcomes us. Only the sound of Christmas carols in the distance somewhere fills our ears. This is us agreeing with our eyes that our fate has been changed, and we will embark on this road together.

"Well… maybe you want to go for a walk?" she suggests.

"Yeah, sure."

"That's good, because I would kind of like the blueberry muffin from Foxy Rox, and I can't go in there because of the coffee smell, so really I'm just going to use you right now."

I grin and stand then offer her my hand. Her delicate fingers plant on my palm, the mere touch a spark, but I ignore it. Gripping her hand, I yank her up. "I can accept that."

A few minutes later, I emerge from the coffee shop, and she is busy scrolling on her phone but slides it into her bag when she sees me.

"Here you are." I hand her the muffin, which she grabs with gusto and fishes into the paper bag.

"My hero," she gushes before taking a giant bite of the muffin. "I didn't realize that I was so hungry."

I throw my thumb over my shoulder. "Do you want me to go back and get something else?"

She shakes her head only to lose a little balance, and I'm quick to sweep her arm up to steady her. "Are you okay?"

"Just a little dizzy, I guess."

I look up and down the street and nobody takes notice of us. It had slipped my mind that rumors could fly; we'll need to tamp those down for a while. "How about we get you home. A little rest."

"Okay."

Luckily, she doesn't live too far and walked here. Her apartment is cute, but we'll need more space when the baby comes.

It seems that I'm already assuming we are going to live together.

I have no time to contemplate that, as I need to focus on steadying Gracie.

Back at her place, we both take our coats off, and I help

as she walks to her bedroom then crawls into bed and curls up on her side, pulling the duvet tight.

This is how the other night ended, except I left.

"Want me to get you something? Water?"

"Nah," she mumbles then yawns. "I'm just tired."

"Sure." I'm about to step away, but her hand darts out to grab my wrist, and my eyes slide down because her touch is calming right now. "Want me to stay?" That is the instant thought that comes to mind.

"Yeah. Just for a little. I don't want to be alone."

Without hesitation, I crawl onto the bed and rest on my side behind her. Natural as the air I breathe, I wrap my arms around her. She pulls my arm tighter around her body, and I hear her sleepy sigh.

It's late afternoon, but I can stay even if I don't rest. "I'll be gone when you wake up purely because we have 7am practice tomorrow and my spare clothes are at home. Sleep."

"Yes, Coach," she replies drowsily.

The corners of my mouth tug because the way she says it shoots a different feeling through me. It sounds a hell of a lot better when she calls me that, as opposed to the guys on the team.

"You listen. Good."

She glances over her shoulder and shoots me a glare. "You know that already. That's what put a baby inside of me." She flops her head back down.

I sputter a laugh under my breath.

It's true. She obeys well. But I have a feeling that I'll be following her cues more in the coming months.

Because she has cast a spell over me, my eyes begin to close, because apparently, I'm getting more comfortable than I planned for today.

That's good because I forgot that we have team holiday photos tomorrow, and I fucking hate ugly Christmas sweaters.

And if sweaters are my biggest worry right now, then it means everything else is promising.

# CHAPTER 8
## GRACIE

I'm howling. Or at least it feels like it.

Lainey will think that I've lost my mind. Luckily, she went to the bathroom as I curl over my phone while resting my arms on her kitchen counter. I'm surprised that I found a spot between all of the baking ingredients.

But this is hilarious. Asher sent me a photo of him in a Grinch sweater.



> Tell me that your design skills could come up with a better sweater?

> It's an ugly-sweater shoot. I will never lower my standards to ugly sweaters. But the sweater really brings out your eyes.

I'm not sure who in the team marketing department convinced him to do this, but he looks to be in misery.

We've been texting quite a bit the last week. I wanted to go to the home game the other day, but I was just too beat. Sleep and toast were calling me. Later in the week, I have a doctor's appointment, but there is no way that Asher will be able to make it. The game schedule has them down in North Carolina.

Straightening my posture, I slip my phone back into my purse just as Lainey returns to the kitchen.

"Someone is giddy. Who is sending you texts?" She bumps my arm in passing on her way to the mixing bowls.

"No one special. My brother just sent me this funny photo," I lie.

Why? Because even my best friend has no clue what is happening in my life. While I try to come to grips with my situation, I just want to do it with Asher. It's crazy, considering we don't know one another that well. But I think it's because we need to find our way together, as it's our big change, and for me, the best way is to be in my own little world.

Lainey doesn't seem to blink at my explanation, instead clapping her hands together with excitement as she eyes the bag of flour. "Annual baking night commences."

Circling around the counter, I smile because I do love this tradition. We always bake everything we can possibly think of, then divide them into tins to give to people. She is a master at cookies, whereas I stick to chocolate bars and things with mint. I'm kind of addicted to using candy canes for decoration.

"I can't wait to cut out inappropriate shapes for your sugar cookies." I love doing that to her. She never knows which tin I hide it in. I'm always a little vulgar even for me, and this year it's a dick shape, because I have every plan to hide it in the tin for her neighbor that she thinks is an insufferable human being.

"I hate that tradition," she scolds me and points her wooden spoon in my direction.

I smile brightly at her. "You love me."

"Yeah, I do. Now let's do this."

Our baking is underway, and her son has already flown through the kitchen a few times in the last hour, stealing treats in the process. This time Enzo sticks around and dips his finger into the bowl of cookie dough while Lainey doesn't see.

Such a smart kid. Cookie dough is a blessing from the skies. I grin at him and join him by taking a nearby tablespoon and scoop into the bowl.

"Hey!" She playfully swats her son. "There is raw egg in that."

*Splat.*

My spoon falls into the bowl at record speed. I've studied my do-not-eat-during-pregnancy list and imprinted it into my brain.

Creases form on Lainey's forehead as she notices. "What's up with you? You always eat the chocolate chip dough."

My lips roll in because I realize that cover stories are my new way of life. "You know, I just decided that I'll focus on the powdered sugar for the Puppy Chow." I quickly grab the plastic bag of cereal.

Lainey still seems slightly puzzled, but her son begins to whine that he should get a little bite, and Lainey gives in.

For the next hour we catch up on her saga with her neighbor, Tyler. He's actually a second cousin to Asher, but they don't talk much unless it is hockey. The only thing they have in common is that they are both a bit cold around the edges.

An icy manner is probably why Lainey and Tyler can't stand one another. Except they really do. It's so obvious, and there have been signs lately that they are completely going to find themselves on a road together.

I wonder if that will be me. Maybe my news needs to

wear off before I assess what it means between Asher and me. I should talk to Lainey. She was once unexpectedly pregnant, except now she is a single mom, and it seems that I won't be. Asher is in this. I have to trust in this journey, otherwise there is no chance at all.

I've been listening to Lainey for five minutes about her neighbor as I close a tin of baked goods. I love listening to her and having the distraction of her life predicaments, but holiday magic be damned, she needs help with a push.

My arm darts out, and I hand her a filled tin with a polar bear on it. "Here." She accepts my offering. "I'll stay in case Enzo wakes up, but Tyler is back… so go."

Her nose lifts, hesitant. "And you were thinking I can bring him cookies?"

"Tis the season, Lainey."

"I'm not sure it's a good idea."

I step closer to her, and I tug on her off-the-shoulder t-shirt, fixing it to be even more revealing. "There. Now go say hello."

I already have my hands on her shoulders and turn her in the direction of the door before she can even protest. Then, I basically shove her out the door, closing it behind her.

Sighing in satisfaction as I turn around, I inhale a relaxing breath and soak in the smells from the kitchen. I've been feeling a little better lately. Slowly walking into her living room, I love the cozy feeling with the Christmas tree in the corner, decorated with white lights, and the stockings over the fireplace. I begin to admire the tree closely and observe all the various ornaments.

I pause when I see one of Enzo's first ornaments. My head slants to investigate a little better, with the tips of my fingers ghosting the shapes. It's a little foot, and then there is another one which is a snowflake, and they are all gosh darn cute.

My eyes are entrapped, and I can't drag my sight away. It hits me suddenly. A baby. All the first holidays with a baby. Then there are ornaments from when Enzo was three, then one he made when he was six. Babies grow, and you are parents forever.

We are parents. Asher and I. Me and Asher.

This all feels emotional all of a sudden. Normally, this would be a prime time to drown myself in the chocolate-covered pretzels, but I'm not sure I want to tempt the early pregnancy hormones.

The sound of my phone ringing breaks my spell, and I quickly go to my bag and pull my cell out. Seeing Asher's name, I'm quick to answer.

"Hi," I say softly.

"Hey, I just wanted to check in. It's getting late, but we ordered in, and I'm still with the coaching staff to discuss our new power play approach… which you probably have no clue what I'm saying." I can hear him smiling with his words.

I smile. "It's fine. I'm at Lainey's for our baking night."

"Oh yeah. How is that going?"

Glancing over my shoulder, I quickly look at the tree and lock my eyes on the baby ornament. "Um… fine… it's fine." That maybe didn't sound too convincing. "I'll bring you a tin. I think I mastered the chocolate-mint bars. There are also a few deformed reindeer cookies. Or perhaps the coconut bars," I list then realize the obvious. "I'm rambling, sorry."

He chuffs a laugh. "I noticed. It's okay, and yes, I love all of that, so count me in. I'm kind of surprised you aren't dying from nausea there."

I walk to the kitchen island and flop onto a stool while I pick up a peanut butter blossom cookie with no intention of eating it. "It's okay today, only once or twice did I struggle, but Lainey didn't seem to notice. Only looked at me funny when I didn't eat the cookie dough, which to be honest was brutal for me because I love that stuff."

"Violins are playing for you. I'll make you cookie dough from chickpeas."

"Eww." I cringe.

"Nah, it's good. You flavor it. The guys make it because it's packed with protein."

I shake away the thought of how that must taste as a quiet moment arrives, and we both linger in our silence for a few seconds.

"You have your appointment. I *really* wish I could be there."

It is disappointing, more than I thought it would be. "I know. It's just the only time the doctor was available, as she is off from next week until the new year. A long vacation, apparently."

"Still… you'll let me know right after how it goes?"

I lift a shoulder and settle for reality and what I need to get used to with his schedule. If my mom could do it, then so can I. "Of course."

"Good. And Gracie… let's talk when I'm back."

That catches me off guard. It sounds serious and scares me as suddenly different kinds of thoughts fly at me from all directions. A negative feeling, if I'm honest.

"Sure." It's a simple reply.

"I've gotta run, but… sweet dreams." There is a gentleness in his voice that causes a ping in my chest.

My mouth slides side to side. "Will do. I have chocolate, after all." I try my best to smile but something feels uneasy, and I can't pinpoint it.

When we end the call, I take a few moments to search for my thought but can't find it.

So, I do what any normal person would do in the month of December; I grab a gingerbread cookie and shove it in my mouth.

THE YOUNG DOCTOR smiles at me as I lie back on the exam table while she looks at her tablet. My blood work came back fine, as I thought it would. "You said it was only one time, which means the conception date is clear, and that really helps us determine how far along you are."

"Yep." I smack my lips together. "On the Monday night before Halloween, as it was a no-practice day, so the coach actually had a normal dinner out, and that matters because the father of this baby has a schedule from hell that I really don't like right now, but I need to deal with it. Throw in Chrismukkah and we can add to my level of crazy right now." I'm a little feisty today, and the poor doctor is on the receiving end of my rant.

She raises her brows at me. "Everything okay? It's important to keep stress levels down."

I rub the back of my neck and exhale a long breath. "Yeah, it's fine. Sleep has just been funny lately." My mind can't seem to stop reeling.

"That is perfectly normal," she assures me. "Anyhow, I'll put you at a July 18th estimated due date."

I sit up on my elbows because there is a bright side. "Oh, that's good. The off-season. Even if the Spinners make it to the championship, then they are finished by then."

"Happy to hear. This also means you just entered about nine weeks, and we can do an ultrasound."

My cheeks hurt from how big the smile is on my face. "I was hoping you would say that." Then my face falls. "I guess Asher can come next time."

She rolls over the cart with the machine. "Look at it this way. There will be many moments that just you and the baby will experience together. It's biology, after all. This is one of those moments, and it is a great way to start your journey."

I think about it for a beat, and she's right. "Yeah, it is."

A minute later with everything set, I'm staring at the screen as the doctor searches the screen and moves around the wand. For a second, I worry, but then the little pulsing dot appears, and then the small form of a baby.

"There you are. He or she is right there." She points with her finger then presses a few buttons on her keyboard and the room fills with the sound of the heartbeat. A swooshing wave on repeat.

The tingle in my eyes is from the happy tears pooling and beginning to fall. My hand covers my mouth because I'm overwhelmed, and I think my cry might turn into a full-on waterfall.

"That's a baby." My own heart is pattering fast from the mixture of nerves and excitement.

She pinches her lips together, amused by my word choice, but she must have heard far worse. "A healthy baby." Her mouse on the screen begins to take measurements. "I'll print a few pictures, and I can record a video to put in the app that lists your appointments."

"Yes, please do," I respond eagerly.

This is all too real now. The final confirmation. A baby is on the way, and I have a million things to figure out.

Maybe that is why I'm stuck in a daze of awe as I walk out of the doctor's office. Staring at my phone, the video of the ultrasound causes the corner of my mouth to kick up. My thumb swipes the screen to pull up Asher's name, and I attach the video.

> I guess we need to start investigating skates for babies, if that's a thing. ;)

Asher is busy between practice, media, and games, but he told me that he checks his messages spontaneously. I'm pleasantly surprised when I return home and my phone pings. One look at my screen, and I gush.

ASHER

So, this is happening.

I frown because that wasn't the response that I was expecting. It's difficult to read emotions through text, but his reply doesn't feel right, and I can't seem to shake it off.

MY EYES MEET ASHER'S, and it is intense, he is completely unreadable. It's almost unnerving. He doesn't break our locked gaze as I follow him into his house. He walks backwards and I walk forward, and my heart races.

Maybe I shouldn't have sent the video, as it's better to see it in person together, but I was too excited and couldn't wait.

But now?

Maybe it's all too real for him.

We end up in his living room, and I can't help but let my eyes wander around the room. I'm pleasantly surprised. It's a big and modern lake house that actually has warmth, with mostly cream-colored furniture.

I sit down on the L-shaped couch and set my purse next to me. He stays standing, and it has me slightly freaking out.

"Do you resent me?" It bursts out of my mouth.

He is taken aback, and his face squinches from severe confusion. "What?"

"Well, you seem… just if the video was too confronting and you resent me for screwing up your career or you are having doubts, then say it now, because I just want to rip that bandage off and leave."

He scratches his cheek right above his day-old stubble. "I'm going to pretend I didn't hear that sentence, and yeah, I probably look like shit, and I'm pretty pissed off that we lost a talented rookie due to a concussion, but…" Quickly, he sits on the coffee table in front of me to ensure that our bodies are squared to one another. "You have nothing to do with any of that, and the best part of last night was seeing that video."

Lines form on my forehead because I'm confused. "You just seem a little out of sorts."

He rubs his face with both of his hands. "Most say I'm aloof, others say I'm approachable, depending on the day. I'm just, wow… overwhelmed." The faintest of smiles appears, and all of my worries disappear. "I mean, this is real. That heartbeat is real."

I smile widely. "It is."

He scoops up my hands to hold them in his palms which feels comforting. "Which is why you are moving in here."

His adamant tone and serious face throw me off. "Wait, what?" My eyes flutter as I double-check that I heard him right.

"You're moving in here. It's simple."

My mouth opens but goes dry, and my eyes remain the size of saucers. "Ha-ha."

"I'm serious."

Geez, no wonder he is a coach. He's demanding, and his penetrating gaze… damn, his eyes are making me melt in places that will not help us in this moment.

"I get that now."

I yank my hands away from his and dig into my bag next to me on the couch to pull out his tin of cookies. Opening the tin, I throw a cookie into my mouth to deal with my bewilderment of this conversation. Then I stuff another cookie in, only to drop the half-eaten baked treat back into the tin because my stomach doesn't like this method of dealing with important decisions.

"I mean, there is going to be a baby, and we would eventually have to address the living situation for the little living human, but now? It's a little fast." I wipe a crumb from the corner of my mouth.

"In regards to the living situation. You're right. Your address is here. Now." He smiles, confidentially contrite.

I shake my head once because I'm still in disbelief of this change of events. "Humor me, how does that work?"

Sinking back into the sofa, I cross my arms, but he rests his hands on my thighs and it's rewiring my body. A pulsing sensation forms between my legs, too.

"Gracie, we have a hell of a lot to figure out, but our time and schedule are not on our side. We need to be ready. Live with me, and then it is easier to get to know one another more and prepare for the baby. I have plenty of space. Plus, over my dead body are you staying in your apartment where you keep a key under a plant."

"Okay, I just move in and then…" He looks at me as though I'm asking a stupid question. I feel the need to clarify. "I sleep…" It draws out of me, as I'm hoping he finishes the sentence.

"In my bed."

I swallow because he's blunt, and I am not complaining about that answer, even if it probably isn't that smart.

He bounces his shoulders. "It's not crazy. We made a baby."

But are we together or is it just physical or am I literally sleeping in a bed? Questions, questions, questions.

His hands squeeze my thighs near my knees, and it's firmness that causes a sensitive sensation to run up my spine to my nipples.

"Gracie, it's better to navigate this closer together. You know I'm right."

Logic floats into my brain for a second, and it makes sense. "I get it."

"Before we know it, hiding a baby secret won't work. Let's not make it more complicated."

My lips purse, and I try to steady my breathing because he is taking over my body and he has no clue.

My nose tips up as I look at him with skepticism. "We only know one another's body. We barely know one another."

His lips are terse and his face turns neutral. "Fine. Ask me some questions."

I drop my arms. "Thoughts on hot chocolate?" *Yeah,* because that's very critical info right now. Geez.

"Disgusting." But a good answer.

"Mistletoe?" Not exactly *not* body related.

"Not needed unless used as foreplay when I already have you naked and we are going into another round," he volleys back.

I attempt to shake away the image, but my body is already liquid. "Soup?"

"For weaklings. Cheesy popcorn?" he counters.

We both shudder from the thought.

"Fine. We have the basics. What about something with substance. We both have ambition, that we have in common.

But for me, I'm not on the road nor have an agonizing schedule. How did you see yourself in a year before all of this and how do you see it now?"

He sighs and glances to the side before driving his sight back to me. I sense that he wants to answer with only honesty. "I'll adapt. Maybe this is a challenge, but we have to be in it together. We are more alike than we think, and we don't say anything because it's obvious."

"So navigating is something we can agree on, right?"

"It is," he promises.

I tap my nails on the sofa cushion as a few thoughts float in and out of my head. I'm invested in learning about him. "For my research purposes. After a bad game, do you need space, someone to listen, or need a distraction?"

A smirk begins to draw on his face. "You forgot an option." My brows knit together, as I'm clueless. "I'm always thinking about the next one. I'm driven by the future. And I'm beginning to realize in the last few days that my drive to thrive also applies to this kid. When it comes to us..." My body straightens, and I think it is due to the anticipation of the end of that sentence. "I'm not yet sure my response method when it comes to us. You throw me off. Not necessarily in a bad way."

The corner of my mouth pulls into a warm smile. All of his words would ace a test if I had one. "Fine. I'll start moving things in after Christmas and Hanukkah. It's already going to be eight crazy nights, so let's not add a move to the equation."

His smirk is full of satisfaction that he won.

And I'm totally screwed because he swoops up my wrist and his thumb is now brushing along my pulse point, while his eyes pull me in.

"It's kind of depressing that you don't have a Christmas tree or menorah here," I say blankly, and I have no clue why that flew out of my mouth, but I'm truly mesmerized and can't even blink.

"That is the least of our worries right now but feel free to fix that."

"Right. Because we're having a baby and I just agreed to move in with you, so that is clearly the pressing matter in this moment."

His eyes dip down, and his two long fingers on his right hand drift to my stomach. The feeling of his fingers touching my belly is pure affection on his part, but I can't help feeling that this is the man that will be so much more than a baby daddy.

The holidays suddenly feel extra magical.

And the room is getting very warm.

Burning-hot warm.

"Are you okay?" Asher looks at me concerned, and he must notice.

Warm. Painful. Aching.

I struggle to relax my body, because I'm tense with arousal. I attempt to scoot away to distance myself. "You know… just a little warm." I'm clenching my thighs together to control my frustration.

"Shit. What's wrong? Let me get you a cloth." Is he that oblivious?

I grab his arm to stop him from leaving. "I'll be fine. It will pass," I lie. "My body has just been notifying me that your touch does strange things to me. So why don't you eat a goddamn snowman cookie while I come to terms with that challenge."

He bubbles a laugh then rolls his lips in to observe me for

a few seconds. His tongue glides along his teeth, only to reveal an almost a cocky grin before he listens and grabs a cookie from the tin.

A peanut butter blossom with red and green sprinkles.

Good choice.

y arm lying above my head is sore, and I begin to move on the sofa, my eyes heavy as they open. It takes mere seconds for me to realize that Gracie is still in my hold, and we must've fallen asleep.

My other arm is wrapped around her waist, and my hand has gravitated to her still-flat belly at some point. The corner of my mouth tugs because underneath my palm is a baby. One that was not on my holiday wish list a few weeks ago.

Gracie begins to stir in my arms and yawns as she wakes. "Did I fall asleep?" she mumbles groggily.

"Mmm-hmm," I answer her and begin to sit up, and she follows.

She rubs her eyes and latches her view onto me. "You too?"

I glance at my watch and it's almost eleven. "Yeah." *With you in my arms.*

"Oh. Well, I should probably get home."

I snicker as I stand because of every ridiculous word in that sentence. "It's fine. You can stay here. I have to get up early for practice, but you can sleep in."

She stands and wiggles her finger side to side. "No. I'm at the boutique tomorrow. There will be no sleeping in, as it will only tip off my mom. I so much as sneeze and she is diagnosing me with health options."

Rubbing the back of my neck, I have to point out the obvious. "I guess we wait for our parents to find out. Probably at some point we should at least mention one another's names to them to ease them into this before we drop the big baby news."

Her head nods as she yawns again. "You are totally right."

"Come on, let's go to bed." I indicate with my head. "I'll give you a shirt if you want."

A droll smile ghosts her lips.

"What? It makes sense," I justify.

Her head tilts to the side. "This is totally not a smart idea, but fine, sure."

Do I need to spell it out? I step closer to her, and her lips part when I extend my hands and plant them on her cheeks, my thumbs drawing circles on her soft skin. "I'll make it easy for us. I'm going to kiss you now."

I pull her to my mouth. It's the instinct of my body; logic was buried deep a long time ago. But Gracie doesn't pull away, even when my tongue seeks entrance, and she eagerly meets me. The way her lips are equal parts soft and firm have me wanting more. Kissing her is a reminder of that night, but I want to kiss her again in this moment too.

Maybe I need to know every little thing about her inside and out. She's the mother of my child, after all. This woman isn't just anyone; she's turned my world upside down since the moment I met her. We have a road to discover, but I'm going to wheel us forward a bit. And I wasn't going to wait to kiss her again.

I barely create a little space as my breath catches in my

throat. It's a whisper of air, but the distance between us feels too far. I sense a measured rise and fall of her chest as her breath is audible and warm.

"Was that okay?" I murmur.

"More than." Her soft cracking voice confirms my thought.

I lean in, and she meets me halfway. There is a strong magnetic force between us. I feather her lips with mine, only to kiss her fervently. My hands don't need a map and find their own way to her lower back to keep her steady, and her arm encircles my middle.

What was supposed to be a simple kiss has turned into a moment where I'm lost. When we part again, our foreheads press in a gentle meeting. This isn't me. I'm not used to this delicacy.

Standing back, I peer down and search her eyes for what she is thinking in this moment. My thumb glides along her swollen bottom lip while I take pleasure in throwing her off her axis. I'm quite confident this isn't how she thought tonight would go.

"I take it you still find me attractive then," she rasps, fighting a smile.

Grinning, I admire her ability to be unreadable because I have no clue if she is playing with me or if she actually had doubts.

"I would say so," I confirm.

She squints one eye at me. "Not just because of the baby?"

"Not because of the baby. Although I'm the one who put a baby inside of you, and when you start to show, I might enjoy you a little extra." The image is sexy as fuck and causes a wild and protective surge.

Her laugh feels good. It's light and swims through me. "Now let's go to bed," I direct.

"Lead the way."

Which is what I do. We spend the next few minutes getting ready for the night. I always have extra toothbrushes from my travel kits from hotels, and I give one to Gracie along with a t-shirt. Letting her have a few moments, I wait in my bed and sit against the headboard.

I never sleep with a shirt on, and I enjoy the idea of Gracie struggling because our bodies are too close. It's not that I'm a presumptuous arrogant ass, it's more that it can't be denied the mood when we are around one another or the tension between us which most definitely isn't negative and can be popped with physical touch. I'd be lying if I said I wouldn't love to go down on her because my cock already imagined it this morning in the shower, but I'll follow her lead.

And that leads straight to Gracie appearing from the bathroom and lifting her leg slightly as she leans against the door frame. She is displaying my shirt with her legs bare. Fuck me, I'm on Santa's naughty list, and if there is a Hanukkah equivalent, then I just went on that list, too.

"This is comfortable, *but* I have one problem." She slowly strides toward me as I sit up taller and adjust my legs that are splayed out long in front of me.

My cock is about to be as hard as titanium, and the way she nibbles her bottom lip is a tantalizing tease. "Oh yeah? What might that be?"

She arrives at the end of the mattress only to begin crawling across the bed with her sweltering eyes that have me at her mercy. "It covers too much skin." Her sensual tone is pure sin. She throws her leg over one side of my lap to straddle me, her arms looping around my neck.

"I couldn't agree more."

Sure, we feel things, and no, it isn't exactly clear where our lines are. But right now, in this moment, we both want one another. Sexual attraction has always been us.

"I'm kind of thinking you could keep me warm. Baby, it's cold outside." She pouts her lips, and I smirk at the way this creature on top of me can take action when there is something she wants and throw in a little holiday cheer in the process.

"Well, good thing I can take care of that little problem for you before we sleep. We have a big day tomorrow."

Her thighs clench my hips, and she begins to circle on top of me, in particular my cock. She moves to rest her palms against my bare chest. "Oh dear, you deserve to be relaxed and rested for tomorrow. Big game?"

My arm encloses her waist, and I press her against my body, feeling the curves of her breast underneath my chin as I peer up and the heat of her pussy on top of my groin. "Practice where I won't go easy on them before I drive down to a winery."

"So stressful, a winery. I hope not with a beautiful woman." She is being playful.

"Don't worry. Just my parents and one of their favorite spots, Olive Owl."

Instantly her body freezes, and her face becomes crestfallen. "Wait. What?"

Now I'm confused by her change in mood. "Uh, I had a few hours to spare, so I'm driving down to Olive Owl to see my parents. My dad wants to pick up a tree on the first day of Hanukkah. That's just how they roll." It should be a quick forty-minute drive tops down to Bluetop, another small town.

Her tight uneasy chuckle under her breath is alarming. "Funny thing. Totally not. You see, I'll be there tomorrow." My forehead creases, as she isn't making sense until she swats my shoulder. "Olive Owl is owned by the Blisswoods, and guess what…"

"What?"

"My brother. Remember I mentioned him once or twice? He's pretty much my mom's age, which is why the stepmom thing gets kind of weird." She shakes her head to stop her from going off track. "Beside the point. My brother is married to a Blisswood, and he runs the winery too. Hence, why I'll be there tomorrow, as I was going to see him and my nieces."

She peels herself off of me and bluntly pulls the duvet to snuggle under because our little predicament has ruined our mood.

"This means you and I will be in the same spot at the same time as my mom and dad and your brother. I need to mention you to my parents, and then when we're ready, we'll inform them in a few weeks that they will be grandparents."

She blows a raspberry and sinks into my bed as though this has always been her bed. "We're adults, we can handle it. Just two people who know one another at the same place and harboring the same secret."

I join her lying down to stare at the ceiling. "Now my stress level is elevated, if I'm honest."

"It will be fine, I'm sure." She hooks her leg over my hip as she moves to her side and scoots into me. "As much as destressing by fucking each other's brains out would be the best solution, I think I just want to sleep now. Talking about our family felt like a cold shower to the mood."

"I can't argue with that."

Wrapping my arm around her and pulling her closer, I at least take pleasure in the fact that I have her in my arms for the rest of the night.

# CHAPTER 10
## ASHER

Biting my inner cheek, I listen as my parents debate the holidays, as they do every year. We're at Olive Owl, sitting inside where the fire is cozy and the wine is the perfect tingle on the tongue, and I attempt to focus on the charcuterie board, but it fails.

"I just thought for one year, we could get a tree with a little more oomph." My mom motions with her hands, her dark hair flowing. I'm going to assume she is talking about the lack of needles on the tree. Even as an adult, I try to make it for their tradition of picking out a tree. The schedule normally doesn't allow it, but this year there was a small window.

My dad grins as he takes a sip of his white wine. "You are just going to go on ornament overload before adding the menorah tree topper. The tree is only the base, we're fine."

Sometimes, I get the impression that he picks out the ugliest tree on purpose. A sort of tongue-in-cheek method of teasing my mom.

My mom brings her hands together and smiles as she seems to look off into the distance. "I still remember the moment when we were searching for a tree and your dad only realized that I was part Jewish when I informed him how I decorate to incorporate Chrismukkah. Funny, right? We were already married, and he didn't know—"

"I know, I know. Married for convenience. Fell in love here. Had me and then decided I was a decent child, so then decided to try your luck with another and got a wild child instead. Yep, heard the story many times," I unenthusiastically list because I hear this story every year.

My dad chuckles, amused. "Now, now, Shaw isn't exactly wild, just… a little unruly at times. Also, let your mom enjoy this day. She bought a bucketload of new ornaments at the winter market out in the suburbs then decided she would take photos of dreidels in funny places to frame and hang on the wall near the tree."

This all sounds on brand for her. I wouldn't expect anything less.

I'm lucky that they are laidback people. Despite having money, they remain grounded. Sometimes I wonder why I can be a little uptight. It's not from them.

She swats his arm as she smiles ear to ear. "Hey, this is the one time of year that isn't boating season where you leave business at the office. That's why you've been so happy today picking out a tree. You did it at record speed, so it must have been love at first sight."

"Or I wanted to finish that part of the day as quickly as possible," he mumbles, and my mom gives him her warning eyes.

"Why don't you two stop quarreling about a tree that will die in two weeks and ask your son how he is?" The fact that I'm volunteering my demise is beyond my comprehension, but I have got to start somewhere. I can't stay too long, as the team is having a morning skate before our last game before the break.

My mom's dark red lips stretch. "You are completely right. My first-born child deserves all of our attention." I smile tightly at her. "What else is new with you? We've only talked hockey since we dragged you across the tree section of the farm. I love this place. You know your dad and I used to visit here on weekends—"

I cut that right off and wince. "Don't need the details again. Especially in the course of ten minutes. I'm still getting over being traumatized due to your attention to details." Even I'm able to make a joke out of this. I'm already getting a little worn out from how happy my mom is right now. It's a good thing, but it takes energy.

My dad shrugs and smirks. "I never ask about your dating life, but if I did, then we would merely suggest this as a top-notch location for booking a room."

I shift uncomfortably in my chair and stretch my neck as this might be my entry point, although only kind of. "Well, my dating status is… well… uhm… may be changing." My voice squeaks.

My mom instantly plants her elbows on the table and rests her chin on her palms. "Do tell."

"You see…" What to say?

"Oh, I recognize that woman." My dad ignores me and peeks over my shoulder.

My sight whips to the corner where Gracie just walked in, stopping because the man next to her just got pulled to the side by an employee. I assume he is her brother because I notice a few facial similarities, although his hair is darker, and seems like the guy in the photo at her place. Shit. Her eyes briefly meet mine, and I see a glimpse of panic for a second. I'm not supposed to be here. It was chopping down a tree and then maybe a drink before rushing on out. Instead, my parents convinced me to stay longer, and my stomach was growling for cheese and crackers, anyhow.

My mom swings her gaze to her side. "Yeah, she was at one of the games. We briefly chatted over her mother's design skills. You know, I even took their family photos when she was a baby. Grace, yep, that's her name."

"Gracie." It pops out of my mouth, and they both look at me. "Her father is a major sponsor," I explain.

"Ah, that's why she was there," my father notes before perusing the board for his favorite cheese.

However, my mom takes it upon herself to wave her hand in the air. It grabs Gracie's attention, and she seems to doubt that the attention is for her. She even searches around her for someone else, anyone else. Reluctantly, she says something to her brother who is in conversation with the staff. Gracie throws on a smile that only I would recognize as fake as she walks to our table. She has got to notice my face full of nerves because I feel my cheeks hurt and my body has a racing heartbeat.

"Hello," she politely greets my mom.

"It's good to see you again. You know, I forgot to tell you last time at the game that it's a small world. I took your baby photo with your parents all those years back."

Gracie seems surprised and strangely steals my attention because it feels like the twilight zone.

"What a coincidence." Gracie laughs nervously deep in her throat.

"Do you have a few minutes? Sit with us. I would love to gush over your mom's upcoming spring collection. I notice more designs are from you."

Gracie's eyes search mine for a clue of what to do, but my

mom holds her friendly smile, and I know Gracie is too kind not to be courteous.

She swallows and returns the unnerving smile as she pulls out the spare chair. "They are. I only have a minute or two. I need to check on my cousins. They have a new horse."

"I'm not one for horses." My dad is a man who loves to sail; farm life isn't for him.

Scooting my chair over, Gracie slowly sits down. I notice how tense she is, and her lips press tight as she still attempts to smile.

"How lovely that you are here," Gracie says, making conversation.

My mom grabs the wine bottle on the table to top up her glass. "Always. It's tradition, and my son managed to take some time to actually take part in holiday cheer."

"Mother, you morph Christmas and Hanukkah together with a goal to outdo yourself on the creative front every year. Remember when you set up that elf along with this Mensch that always sat on a bench. You put them together on a beach in Hawaii, with sand on the kitchen table one holiday season?" I deadpan.

She waves me off. "You were ten and it was cute."

Gracie tilts her head to the side and quirks her mouth as though she thinks it's an adorable idea. "Sounds like my mom and dad. We had a dreidel drinking game the year I turned 21 and ended up playing pin the carrot on the snowman at two in the morning. Memorable, I guess."

My mom glows with joy. "Another Chrismukkah family. I love it. See, Asher, relatable." She winks at me, and I know what's crossing her mind.

Gracie notices too. But the moment dies down, and an odd silence floats around us. It's indescribable.

"Well, I'm sure you want to catch up with your family,

and I don't want to keep you long." I give her a route to escape.

She glances at me before returning her awkward smile to my parents. "Yes. Horses and cousins." She swallows. "I'm sure I'll see you a lot more." *Oh no.* "I mean, at the games and all." Maybe a save. "Not like there would be any other reason." This doesn't feel good. Gracie can ramble, and I fear we are entering that dangerous territory. "I'm pregnant." It spills out of her mouth, and she immediately freezes from her own astonishment that the words just escaped her lips. "Did I really just say that?" she whispers to herself.

"Yep," I confirm.

Well, here we are.

"Congratulations." My mother hasn't connected the dots yet. However, the silence and Gracie's visibly rapid chest begin to cloud the table.

I feel my face tighten, and my jaw flexes side to side in my best attempt to gather composure for what is about to come.

My mom notices, and her smile wilts as she tries to dissect what's happening.

Ah, hell.

She swings her gaze to me and then back to Gracie and returns to me. "Oh." It comes out mundanely. It takes a few moments before her entire appearance changes with her eyes turning into saucers. "O*hhhh.*"

My mom totally gets it now.

"We're pregnant," I clarify.

My father looks between us all and lifts a shoulder. "Okay."

My mom brings her hand up to cover her mouth, but her smile is too wide to cover. "You're pregnant."

"Shh," I hiss and scan the room.

Gracie appears panicked as she searches my face for an answer to her plea of what to do.

"Her family has no clue," I whisper.

My parents nod gingerly in understanding.

"I'm sorry, it just came out," Gracie apologizes to me in a hushed tone.

"Surprising. But great news," my father whispers. He is too casual for this earth-shattering moment, but that's just him, unless it's a business deal that he needs to be cold-blooded for.

"I didn't realize that you two were dating," my mom leans into the table to ask quietly.

Gracie and I both look at one another and shrug. "It's not exactly…"

My mom raises her hand in the air to stop us. "Say no more. I got it," she whispers. "When is the baby due?" she mouths.

"July. It's still early in the pregnancy," Gracie loudly whispers.

"We get it. Lips are sealed," my father assures her in a loud mutter.

My mom reaches out to touch Gracie's arm on the table. "But this is a Hanukkah and Christmas gift rolled into one. On the first night, too. You know, isn't it great how Hanukkah falls with Christmas week this year. July is a good month. She'll be the right size for cute baby holiday clothes next year. Just squeeze her little cheeks," she coos in a loud whisper that I'm sure the table next to us could hear.

I shuffle my chair closer to the table. "Here comes the crazy. Only two minutes in and you're planning out our kid's future. And we don't know if it's a girl." My hushed voice is sharp with frustration.

My mom is not impressed with my comment. "Excuse me

for being excited for the fact that I'm going to be a grand-mother, and I still look smoking, so I won't be one of those old-looking grandmas." She's returning to her shouting mutter.

Gracie runs her fingers through her hair and claws her sides. "We look like idiots talking like this. I see my brother puzzled over in the corner as he observes," she utters to me.

Sliding my gaze over my shoulder, I see her brother talking to a waiter, but his eyes remain fixed on our table.

Whipping my sight back, I feel my eyes enlarge. "Can we keep this news at our table? I didn't plan on anyone from Gracie's family murdering me today," I say tightly.

My dad has a serious face when all of his attention lands on me. "Don't be silly. They need you alive. For the baby and all." He has an undertone of humor. What the hell is this conversation?

"If you will excuse me, I think I need to leave. I'm sure Asher can finish this discussion," Gracie says in a low voice and gives me a weak smile.

I touch her hand as she stands. "They will keep this all under wraps, don't worry," I promise.

She nods like she believes me before she looks at my parents. "I'm sure we will get to know one another a lot more now."

"Of course. We'll have dinner when things are a little calmer." My dad provides logic to this conversation.

As Gracie turns, my mother speaks up. "Ginger. Lots of ginger. Oh, and send me photos."

I roll my eyes. "Run, Gracie, run."

She walks away, but I feel heavy eyes on me. Turning in my seat, I face my parents.

"Well, this is news." My dad's neutrality is appreciated,

proven by the fact that he cooly inspects the glass of wine he is holding.

My mom leans back to rest against the chair, and she crosses her arms. "Huh. I didn't see this coming, but…" She shrugs. "Mazel tov. Now, will you pass the bread?" She too has returned to earth as though the last five minutes didn't happen.

I'm relieved in one way. Another item off the checklist of preparing for the shift our lives are about to take.

Drifting my gaze to the entrance of the room, I see Gracie looking tensely at her brother, and I hate saying it while she's stressed, but she is glowing and still beautiful. She survived meeting my parents, and that gives me comfort that she and I can be a team. The kind that has nothing to do with hockey, instead our personal lives. The part of life that actually matters. A career is temporary, but your relationships with others are forever.

We're connected, and it's up to us to figure out in what way.

# CHAPTER 11
## GRACIE

My brother stops in the middle of the parking lot with the barn on one side and the inn on the other, and Christmas lights all around nearly blinding me. He is an outdoorsman which means it doesn't bother him that it's a bitter chilly winter night. Drew is technically my half-brother, but to me, that never crosses my mind. The age difference is vast, which means sometimes I feel like I have a brother and other times two dads.

He crosses his arms and juts his chin out. "What the hell was that?"

I laugh weakly. "What?" I play dumb.

He stares at me blankly. "Don't play cute. You and the hockey coach in a battle of whispers. Something I need to know?"

"Nope." I tear my eyes away and find a focal point on the stuffed life-size Santa Claus sitting on a tractor.

"Really? Funny thing is that I've known you since birth, and I know when you are lying. So, what? Are you seeing that guy or something?"

Popping my lips repeatedly isn't helping me in this situation. "Not exactly."

"Okay, then it's no problem that I mention to Dad that my little sister was in an odd situation and thought he might be curious to know."

"Don't!" That sounded far too vigorous. My eyes slice straight through him because he just walked me straight into his trap.

Drew's eyes grow big. "There we go. Something *is* going on."

I notice my breath misting in the air because it's freaking beyond cold. "Can you just let it go for now?"

He steps back and assesses my stance for what seems like an eternity. "No." His brows furrow as he studies me more. "No way." I'm surprised by his sudden choice of words. Then I remember that his wife belongs to the Blisswood family and there is barely a time that a woman in that family isn't pregnant. He doesn't need to study me long to figure out the root of my nerves. An almost devilish smirk formulates on his mouth while he rubs his fingers over his chin. A rumbled laugh in his throat is concerning. "Pregnant, huh?" He whistles. "Dad and Piper are going to love this news about their little princess." He takes pleasure in this but not in a malicious way, that's just not in him.

I step to him and stand tall. "You. Will. Not. Tell. Them," I urge.

He raises his hands up. "Oh, don't you worry. I'm leaving that all to you."

I huff a breath because this night is not happening. Every plan that was formulated in my head has failed. First, with Asher's parents and my careless slip, and now my brother knows my news, too.

His enjoyment from my unexpected news that my dad

most definitely will flip out over is cooled to pure affection. "If you are happy about this then I'm happy about this." The honesty in his face warms any heart, always has.

My body eases, and I can't help but break out in a smile. "I am. I really am. Almost done with the first trimester, so I guess my accidental confession to Asher's parents and you are not so bad."

He touches my shoulder. "You'll be a good mom. You're a great aunt." His twin girls are only a few years younger than me, but when they were babies and I was eight, I treated them like living dolls.

"I think so too."

Drew glances to the side when he hears a kid yell out to his parents as they enter the tree area. "And you and the coach…?"

I shrug. "I don't know."

He chuckles to himself. "I'm going to have to point out that you are your parents. Your mom fell for a coach."

My brows bounce up then fall down. "Thanks for that reminder."

"Hey, you may be an adult, but I still get to tease you, Miss Family Tradition."

I roll my eyes. "You're right."

"Is it really bad if I ask if we can have a bet to see how long it takes for Dad to say that Asher has to marry you?" He's dead serious.

I brush him off with a scoff. "Don't be ridiculous." I pause. "Three minutes."

"Three seconds," he challenges.

I lift my chin out. "What do I get if I win?"

"I'll make you the crib *and* a matching rocking chair."

Game on. Because he is great at carpentry.

"Deal. And if I lose… I'll tell your wife that I absolutely

*need* you at Easter at Dad's because I'm pregnant and emotional and can't handle matza for our five-minute Passover Seder that follows." He loves Lucy and would do anything for her. But he also deserves some quiet, and any holiday with the Blisswood family is a headache even for the experienced souls.

"I accept this bet." We smile at one another. "Now let's hug it out, and let me know the code word that the Senior Coach has learned the news that he's going to be a granddad again and might ask me for tools to contemplate murder."

Accepting his open hug, I'm reassured. He gives me a moment to remember everything is fine and it can only get more exciting, even if it's daunting.

I PEER over my mom's shoulder as I watch her sketch a design for a gorgeous long nightgown that will have soft see-through mesh and slits up both legs. Sophisticated yet provocative at the same time. Of course, comfortable as can be.

Lately, while drawing my dress designs, I've been focusing on her cozy pajamas that are for any occasion. Pajamas are popular during the holidays here in the boutique. Her entire brand is by no means small, but the boutique is where the magic happens. Plus, Piper Crews is friendly to everyone and takes the time to talk to customers. Not many fashionista powerhouses do that.

"You doing okay? You seem distant lately," she asks but continues drawing. As much as she is excellent at all of the design programs on her computer, she is traditional and prefers to draw by hand just like me.

Stepping to the side, I pick up a piece of satin cloth next

to the jar of candy canes mixed with chocolate gelt coins to keep my hand occupied. "Totally. Just tired."

Abruptly, she sets her pencil down and swivels on her stool to face me. "Are you feeling okay? There are a lot of flus going around. Or is it the fact that your dad nixed my idea to invite the rabbi for Christmas dinner where we do charades?"

I snort a laugh. "Although the fact you even half joke about that is concerning… No. It's not that." Debating what to say, I can honestly say that I haven't rehearsed a word.

My mom doesn't say anything, instead waiting patiently.

"Can I tell you something and you won't say anything to Dad? Not yet anyhow. Maybe this is the year to get that new puppy since Clove passed away. It will keep Dad distracted."

Her eyes grow with wonder. "No puppy," she says bluntly. Also code that she's waiting and I'd better give her an explanation pronto.

I take a big inhale, ready to do this. "The thing is, something unexpected has happened."

"As in?"

Clearing my throat, I pep myself to say the sentence that will change my mom's world. "Hopefully, you see it as a Chrismukkah gift rolled into one." Her look is stern that I better speed this up. "I'm pregnant."

She goes still, not entirely sure what to do or say, and she stays this way for a few moments. "With whom?" There is neither disappointment nor excitement in her voice.

"The coach of the Spinners," I answer simply.

She nods repeatedly and a smile slowly etches on her face. "Ah, I saw him outside with you once. You both looked enchanted with the other, and now you're pregnant."

"Yeah."

"My baby is having a baby." She grabs my wrists to yank me closer so she can hug me. "I knew it."

I retreat my head back, bewildered. "How?"

She lifts a shoulder. "A sixth sense."

"Okay, well, now you know, and I'm due in July," I intone.

She brushes my hair with her fingers as though I'm still a child. "How are you feeling?"

"Not too bad. A little extra tired and nauseous sometimes. Maybe it's my withdrawal from holiday cookie dough, though."

She bops my nose with her long finger. "But still, you seem happy, and that means that I'm happy."

I smile at her. "I'm excited, and Asher is too."

Her face sours for a second. "*So,* you might want to explain that aspect of this equation."

Shrugging, I step out of her embrace and begin to wander around the high-top table. "It happened, and we are just… figuring things out."

"Okay."

"Okay?" She is letting me off that easy?

My mom walks to her table and picks up her pencil. "Yep. I'm not going to press. As long as he is a stand-up guy then I'll let you two figure things out."

Phew, I feel lighter. "Thank you."

"I guess I'm designing some baby onesie pajamas with little hockey pucks."

I begin to twist the ends of my sleeves around my fingers. "There is just one thing." She looks up at me. "Can you not tell Dad? I need a little time on that front. I'm trying to figure out the right approach."

My mom sighs and pinches the bridge of nose. "Why am I not surprised?"

My stomp back to her must look like a child complaining. "Come on, you know him."

"I don't like keeping secrets… but it is your news to share."

I launch forward and wrap my arms around her for a big hug. "Thanks, Mom."

She backs away and gives me a firm look that she is struggling to give because she just wants to smile. "But you have to tell him ASAP."

"I promise."

She pastes on a bright smile. "Good. How about you invite the father of my grandchild to Chrismukkah?" She holds a finger up before I can protest. "I know Asher is free because they have a three-day break over Christmas."

My face falls because she is right. "But Dad always makes us wear Santa hats, and he wears that apron that has an elf holding a dreidel that says *this elf's favorite drinking game*."

"A great icebreaker, huh."

She's standing her ground, and deep down, I know she's right. Everyone in the family has already discovered my news, and my dad has to be next.

WAITING at the entrance of the practice rink, I'm banking on the fact that a winger went down in practice, so they are taking a break early. Asher spots me right away as he exits the ice and does a double take before he motions to his watch at one of the assistant coaches at the benches. Grabbing his blade guards, he pops them onto his skates before he walks to me.

"Hey, what are you doing here?"

I search around his back to ensure nobody is taking notice of us. "I just wanted to apologize in person about letting everything slip out to your parents. Nice win yesterday, by the way."

"Thanks. And don't worry about it. Life just wanted us to tell them then."

"Well, now my brother and mom know."

His face strains for a second. "And?"

"Both happy."

"Good."

I cringe at the next news I need to deliver. "But funny thing…"

Now he appears uneasy. "I've gotten to know you enough that when you say that, it normally isn't funny at all."

I hum in agreement. "You're not wrong. However, this one there is no option. I can tell my dad by myself—"

"No. I need to be there. It's the right thing to do."

My mouth gapes open, and I tip my hip out to grip. "Really? Now you want to discuss traditional options?"

He rolls his eyes before he steps back to give me room because he seems to notice something. "Yeah, I can sign your cousin's hockey stick."

My face wrinkles "Wha—"

Declan, team owner, appears by my side. "Hello, you two. Didn't expect to see you here, Gracie."

"Just asking for a third night of Hanukkah present that she forgot," he lies.

"Yep. That." I click my fingers and point to Asher.

Declan draws a line with his eyes between Asher and me. There is zero belief in his face, and he sets his sights on Asher. "Well, I'm sure you can sign that gift to make our *sponsor's* daughter happy." There is 100% warning in that tone.

"Don't worry."

Declan squeezes Asher's shoulder in passing. "Great. I'm aware how much you value *thoughtful* actions." Asher winces. "Make sure the guys and all of the team return from the break with a clear head," he calls out as he walks away.

Asher releases a deep breath. "Fuck."

"Let's be honest here. We're unraveling." I'm dead serious.

"No shit." He drags the back of his finger across his jaw. "What were you saying before that interruption?"

Looking away, I can't bear to see his reaction. "You've been invited to Chrismukkah at my parents'."

He sighs and chuckles bitterly to himself. "Well, hopefully Santa delivered some extra holiday cheer and kindness to your dad."

Touching his arm, I forgot how much just touching anywhere on his body sends sensations through me. "I mean, my mom is baking his favorite Yule log dessert and that normally puts him in a good mood. I can ask her to add extra amaretto or rum to the cake this year."

He stares at me blankly. "Please," his reply is flippant.

If the Maccabees had their oil that lasted eight nights, then he will have my alcohol to survive these nights. See? Still in a festive spirit.

# CHAPTER 12
## ASHER

I 'm carrying a fucking poinsettia. That's what my world has come to as I stand outside of Gracie's parents' house. It's large, on a lake, and there is an overzealous number of Christmas lights on the house that could possibly overload the Illinois power grid.

"Okay, just let me do the talking. Now isn't the time for the man-to-man crap. Let me play into the daddy's princess angle." Gracie is more nervous than me as she straightens her hair and exhales deeply. "I'm an adult, yet I feel as though I might disappoint him, but then I remind myself that it's ridiculous. Yet, here I am."

I'm very familiar with the feeling.

Already, we are not starting on the right foot. She could have used her key or walked right into the home she grew up in, but she chose to ring the doorbell then realized her error.

She is bouncing on her feet, attempting to create warmth in her body, and I can see that she is visibly nervous. Looking forward, I see my breath in the air because it is freezing.

"Want to know a secret?" I say, trying to distract her.

"What?"

"I actually kind of like the holidays."

She stops mid-bounce, and her eyes whip to the side. An angelic smile spreads on her rosy cheeks. "Really?" she coos.

"Let's not make a big deal about this." I'm trying to downplay it, but there is some truth in what I said.

"What is it that you like? Is it the songs, the cookies, or maybe a stocking full of coal? Did your parents do that?"

My eyes grow big. "No. Did yours?"

"Oh gosh no." Phew.

"I guess it's the atmosphere. Everybody is in a good mood and there's special food. We always used to get little gifts for every night of Hanukkah. Socks or… well, more socks."

She grabs my arm. "Yours too?" It's working. She seems to be calming down and forgetting the hour ahead.

I can't help it because it seems that I've unlocked a few memories that brighten my mood. "Ties too."

"That sounds like something an old married couple would give to one another," she remarks humorously.

"I would keep that thought to yourself. Not sure parents want to be reminded of age. Anyway, we would also have those donuts. The sufganiyot. My dad is always proud when he manages to remember how to say it. There is a great bakery in the north suburbs that makes the best. Then there is also the fact that we always had a train around the Christmas tree."

"My dad does the same. Okay, so you kind of secretly might like the holidays."

I roll a shoulder back. "Nah."

Silence fills the air, and for a few beats, we are lost in one another's eyes as our smiles fade. "Asher… the holidays are about family, and next year we will have a baby with us."

"Yeah… yeah, we will." The words are flooded with affection.

The door whooshes open which breaks our attention, and Piper Arrows opens the door, slightly perplexed. "What's with the doorbell?"

Gracie is quick to walk into her mom's arms for a hug. "Sorry, I'm out of sorts. Merry Chrismukkah."

Her mom's eyes meet mine as she wraps her arms around her daughter. She knows who I am, but now she has to see me through a different lens. The one where I'm the father of her grandchild… the guy who knocked her daughter up, but I prefer the classy option.

Gracie pulls away, and just like Gracie said, her mom is still smiling at me. "It's good to see you. Crazy news but wonderful."

My arms missile out with the flowers. "Here. These are for you. The Flower Jar had only a few left, so ignore the dying leaf in the back."

She assesses the plant and shrugs. "It's the thought that counts, and besides, nobody will be looking at the flowers once Hudson finds out about the news."

"Joy," I say dryly.

We enter the home, and it's as meticulous as one would think. The interior reminds me of my parents' house in Lincoln Park, except this place is modern and open. I'm also nearly blinded by a giant Christmas tree covered in gold and a train going around at the base.

"That is a monster of a tree," I mutter to Gracie.

"If my mom asks, my great-grandmother's menorah is the star of the show," she says under her breath.

Walking further into the living room, my nerves are hitting me, and I'm on the hunt for any sight of Hudson Arrows.

"There you are. I was getting worried." Right on cue, he walks into the living room with two glasses of sangria in his hand and an apron that says the *Oy vey, it's Santa's day*. His sight lands on me, and my presence seems to throw him off balance. "Coach Tate, I had no idea you were joining us. Welcome."

His festive-cheer bubble is about to break.

Gracie intervenes. "He's here. Now where is that hug?" She opens her arms and heads straight for her dad.

"There's my princess. I've made the roast chicken with rosemary that you like. Did latkes on the side because your mother's grandma will haunt me in my dreams tonight if I don't cook her recipe."

Piper's humorous glare is shot his way. "Cute. Why don't we all sit down."

"Sure. Let me grab some more glasses of sangria," he suggests.

"No!" Gracie is a little overzealous with her interruption. "I mean, I just don't feel like sangria for now. Let's just have a seat. Oh, great, snacks." She motions to the coffee table and already beelines to it.

"Uh, thanks for having me." That's my only line right now.

We all join Gracie who is now stuffing her mouth with crackers, and I'm not sure if it's due to nausea or simply avoidance.

Hudson hands Piper a drink, and she sits on the armrest of the sofa. "The more the merrier. My son and the grandkids only come tomorrow for brunch."

We all sit for a few seconds as her parents sip a drink, and Gracie grabs more crackers. It only draws attention from her father.

"Go easy there. Are you hungry? I can probably speed up the bird." He hitches a thumb over his shoulder.

"Probably just a little carsick," I lie.

Piper places her hand on Hudson's leg, and she gawks her eyes at Gracie and me. Her sign that there shall be no stalling.

"Oh, wait…" His eyes swims between his daughter and me. "Why did you two show up together? Actually, Asher, why are you here?" The man is now purely baffled.

"Storytime," Gracie says, muffled through her cracker chewing, as our announcement entry point.

Suddenly, Hudson's face hardens as he does his best to understand.

"Gracie is pregnant," I burst out. This time I get the point for letting words flow out of my mouth without thought.

One tick. Two ticks. Three. Because he just knows that we are not playing a game.

"Marry her," he firmly states.

Piper's head falls into her hand as though she was expecting this.

"Are you kidding me?" Gracie nearly shouts.

I touch her thigh to calm her. "I'm sorry, it just came out," I explain to her.

"Not you," she clarifies. "My brother actually won the bet that it was three seconds before my dad went all traditional on me."

Hudson stands, clearly agitated. "You." He points his finger at me.

I stand, ready to be the man who directs a team. No fear of opinions. "I need you to relax. We're having a baby and that's that. Gracie is healthy, and we're happy about this."

"A Chrismukkah gift." Piper pulls on Hudson's arm to rein him in.

He looks back at his wife. "No. A proper gift would be my daughter first introducing us to her older beau and then one day he will ask me for her hand in marriage then have a wedding. Then somewhere between the Easter egg hunt and downing ridiculously sweet grape wine at the Seder, they would surprise us with a little onesie in a wrapped box."

Gracie throws her arms into the air. "Well, it's not like that. Deal with it."

Her dad spears his gaze at me. "Yes, it's not like that, so please now do the right thing and marry her."

Piper rolls her eyes and looks frustrated at her husband's level of crazy.

"This isn't the stone age. We don't need to be married." Gracie stands, clearly annoyed.

Straightening my spine and feeling confident with our situation, I'm ready to challenge him. "She's right. But I have no intention of leaving her side. I'm going to take care of her and the baby. In July, you'll have another grandchild, and hopefully, you will be happy along with us."

He lifts his chin, appearing to calm a smidgen. "Of course, I'll be happy that we have a grandchild to add to the Arrows brood. But you two…" He grabs his glass of sangria from the side table next to the sofa and takes the world's longest sip before setting it down. "I didn't even know you two are together."

"Eeeh," Gracie peeps out then tugs my arm. "Just go with it," she informs me under her breath. "We're new. Going slow because of messy schedules and his public life, you know how it goes."

Hudson's eyes grow. "Having a baby isn't slow," he deadpans.

"Well, you better catch up really quick because we're happening," I reiterate.

My brazen attitude takes him by surprise. "You know, I'm excellent at throwing things. That's the whole point of football. Then I have my son who I can borrow things from the farm to throw. Axes would be my tool of choice."

I don't blink once. "And? You're not going to do anything to the father of your grandchild. Especially when he wants to step up."

Gracie walks to the middle of the room and raises her arms on each side as if she needs to keep us apart. "Will you two calm it down a notch? If I need to lie down from exhaustion, I can promise you both that it's from you two and not the baby."

Hudson and I both pin our eyes on Gracie before we square off with hardened stares. I'm on board with Gracie's request. Is her dad?

His jaw stretches to the side, and he is contemplating. "You're right, princess… and… I'm confident that Asher will take care of you and the baby."

A smile emerges on her face. "See? Was that so hard?"

"I think it's a good idea if we can maybe settle and celebrate. Oh…" I point to the menorah with four lit candles on the fireplace mantel. "You know that seems to be a special menorah, very old and classic. A lot of meaning and truly exquisite."

Piper perks up and is elated by my comment. "It is. Everyone talks about Hudson's tree, but really look at it. It belonged to my grandmother Ruth." She splays her hands in the direction of the fireplace.

Gracie turns to me and gives me a thumbs-up that nobody can see for buttering up her mom. "Come on, Dad. Your chicken will get dry if we drag this out."

He bobbles his head side to side and cracks a smile. "My little girl is no longer a little girl." She walks to her dad, and he gives her a side hug. It's heartwarming to see actually. "How are you feeling?"

I follow as they walk side to side, and Piper smiles affectionately at me as she too follows.

"I'm doing well. The baby is due in July."

"The off season. At least something was well planned."

She playfully pinches his arm. "Funny. Now let me tease you about your apron."

The calm after the storm is a welcome relief. A few minutes later we are all sitting at the dining table with food in the middle. The table is elegant, decorated with little details.

Piper pours me a glass of wine. "A shame Drew couldn't join us, but it's his wife's year to be with her family. A few neighbors will stop by later. Of course, we will keep every-thing under wraps until you two are ready."

"Thanks, Mom." Gracie turns to me and squeezes my hand, leaning in to speak into my ear. "We did it. We survived. Another step achieved."

Yeah, we did. Now we can focus on other things: us.

That makes me smile to myself.

Hudson passes me the plate of latkes, but my nose begins to tingle in the process, and I sniff, as do the others. It's smoke.

"Do you smell that?" Piper squinches her nose.

Hudson peers over her shoulder only to bounce up. "Oh no."

I follow his line of sight and instantly follow.

It's the fucking poinsettia on fire. It's a small containable blaze, but we make no mistake that the leaves are lit up. It's on the floor and not close enough to the fire in the fireplace but burning the edge of a stocking with Hudson's name on it.

"What is happening?" Piper sounds panicked.

I feel Gracie and Piper following me, and we all watch Hudson throw a blanket from the sofa onto the plant.

"The candle from the menorah on the mantel, it fell," Hudson explains as he continues to extinguish the smoke and flame.

Gracie touches my shoulder from behind and sputters a laugh. "Kind of funny, no?"

Her father looks at all of us with a serious stare until his gaze lands on his wife. He tips his nose up. "This is your grandmother. She is haunting us already."

Piper struggles to take him seriously. "Why?"

"Piper, you know that your grandmother and I got on famously. But I already know what discussion we need to have."

"Humor me." Gracie is struggling to keep her hysterics in check.

"Circumcision. We should talk about if the baby is a boy. Otherwise, your great-grandmother is going to ensure I have a nightmare tonight."

There isn't an ounce of humor in that sentence.

CLOSING THE PASSENGER-SIDE DOOR, I circle my Porsche and slide into the driver's seat. Starting the car, I turn to Gracie while we wait for the car to warm up. She's resting her head against the headrest and staring at me with a tiny smile and entwines our fingers on the middle console.

"Not going to lie. This evening will go down in my history books," I admit.

She blocks her big smile by biting her bottom lip. "Really? That's surprising. It was just normal conversation. I mean, marriage, fires, circumcision, or if you will pass the ultimate test of installing a baby seat into your family car that you now have to buy."

I glance quickly to the backseat of my sports car. "Your dad might have a point on the car issue."

"All of the other stuff might come up again, but between us and not anytime soon."

We both look down on our joined hands. "The next few weeks we can just focus on us and the little things," I suggest.

"Exactly. I've already started packing a few things for your place. I can't end my lease so fast, but I can start to stay at yours more."

"Good."

It's more than appealing having her at my place every time I return home. No matter the type of day, she brings life and allows me to be carefree for a moment, even if the world around us is full of decisions and pressure.

There are a few seconds of quiet that drift through the car with our eyes tethered. "You know, I'm beginning to realize something about you." Her voice is floaty and quiet.

"Enlighten me."

"Behind the steely coach in a flashy suit, you are actually a family man. Maybe you didn't know, but your mood changes when you are around family. You might come across as annoyed and firm, but inside, you are always smiling. Enjoying the moment. Using it as a reason to forget about the world."

I want to highlight that she's been observing me. Instead, I jump into defeat. "Seems you solved me then." I speak in barely a whisper. "*Or…*" My thumb begins to rub circles on the top of her hand. "All of what you said is because I'm around you."

Her pressed lips draw into a wistful smile. "I think I only noticed because it's what I'm experiencing."

I could have any woman in my bed, but I want her. I've never known addiction until I met her. The instant sight of her lips, a shade of pink roses, and her laugh that is a magnet and every word an adventure.

Now I have the chance to have her. The baby is just a bonus. Maybe that makes me a bad father for not thinking the baby is first and Gracie is the prize. It's just if I close my eyes, it's Gracie I'm beginning to inhale in every breath.

Everything inside of me knew from day one that she was an entrapment, purely from our eyes meeting and something crazy leaving her mouth to tease me. I just thought my life with her in it was unimaginable.

Leaning in, I cup her face with my hands and place a gentle kiss on her lips.

The baby just makes me grateful that he or she pushed me to see Gracie as imaginable.

Our mouths part, but I brush my lips along her jawline, feeling her warm breath and the tug of her fingers curling around my coat lapels. My intention is to lay her down on my bed, but I'm confident that we'll both be too tired, and that's okay. I just need to kiss her for my fix.

But damn, the feeling of her grip and the way her body curves into me will make it difficult for me to drive home without a hard-on. Her mouth follows the outline of my face and travels to my ear.

"There are things that I want you to do to me," she rasps. "But we have got to leave because making out as an adult in my parents' driveway is not what we need right now. Plus, my dad has cameras everywhere and it's just awkward."

There we go.

Hard-on issue no more.

# CHAPTER 13
## GRACIE

The light peeking through the morning clouds streams through the blinds, and it's what is keeping me from drifting away into heaven. Except, I'm already there. I feel Asher's tongue flick my clit, as he is between my legs under the cover.

My hips lift because the sensitivity overload is too much, and I can't lie still. I moan and rake my fingers through his hair. I should be numb from last night, but there is something about morning sex which just hits differently. You're both already naked and you wake ready. It took only one sweep of his finger between my legs, coating him with how much I want him, and he slid down to lick me.

The day after Christmas is always a lazy day, and maybe that feels like we move slower together. Looking down, I meet his eyes as he's watching me, and I'm closer to coming. He holds my thighs wide, his mouth covers me, and the moment his tongue slides inside me, a slew of curses leaves my mouth.

"This is too much." I'm on fire, and my nipples are near painful as I'm so aroused and the cool air in the room keeps them peaked. I'm about to lose it. "Let's switch positions." I guide his head up to make him stop, and there is a smirk on his face that is dangerous.

"What position might that be?" His voice is gruff and hazy with lust.

I yank and push, leading him to the way that I want. Until my mouth is near his cock and his tongue can return to my pussy. There is no further discussion, we both begin to suck and lick one another.

His cock is large but somehow fits perfectly in my mouth. I slide my tongue up and down his shaft, flicking my tongue against his head then slowly tasting. I'd much rather do this to him than a damn candy cane. It's a little hard to focus because of the wicked things that he continues to do to my clit, but I still manage to bob up and down his length.

Our movements mimic one another as we use the tips of our tongues to drive one another wild. He murmurs against my pussy, and I hum with my mouth full. We enjoy one another for a while until he moves.

He leads me to lying on my side, and he enters from behind me. Spooning me, his arm wraps around me, his hand plays with my breasts, and I look over my shoulder so our mouths can fuse together as he pumps in and out of me.

"They're getting big," His voice scrapes as he nips my earlobe.

"There is a reason for that." My voice is breathy, and I interlink our fingers before placing the palm of his hand near my bellybutton.

His lips dragging along my shoulder heighten my body's sensitivity even more.

We move in sync until I begin to shiver and vibrate around his cock inside of me, and my body goes slack as he continues to move until he finds his own escape.

We stay together in our spooning position for a little longer until he finally abandons me, and we both roll to our backs, attempting to calm our heavy breathing.

I'm fighting to keep my body from slipping back into sleep because I'm so relaxed, but Asher informed me last night right before getting me naked that his parents would be stopping by a little later.

"I can't move." I'm exasperated.

Asher is spread out like a starfish on his back. "Give me a minute to recover."

That entire sentence causes me to giggle. "Old man."

He turns his head with one eye closed and the other peeking open to give me a warning.

I gather my strength and roll out of bed, grabbing his button-down shirt in the process to throw on. "Well, you do you, and I'm going to grab some juice in the kitchen."

He forces himself up to sitting and rubs his face. "Okay. The bakery should be stopping by soon." He yawns. "With a delivery of things for lunch with my parents."

"Hmm, yum." I'm banking on an orange roll in that order.

When I'm in the kitchen, I pick up a banana from the fruit bowl then proceed to the fridge. Opening the door, I realize that Asher doesn't have much, but luckily, there are a few juice options. The intercom sounds, which means someone from Jolly Joe's is here with Asher's order. Since Asher is probably getting dressed, I walk to the doorbell screen in the kitchen, and I buzz them in so they can get through the gate at the bottom of the driveway.

I need something to chew on, and I peel the banana before taking a big chomp and debate if I should have a bowl of cereal but remember that there is food arriving. Walking to the front door, I pause before I turn the handle when I realize that I'm only in Asher's shirt, and I growl to myself. But it goes down to my knees and I'm short on time, so that's the best that I can do.

Opening the door, I quickly regret that decision. I'm familiar with the guy with a cocky grin who is in front of me holding a small, blue-and-silver wrapped present. I've just never met him. Tall, a wave of dark hair, similar eyes to the man upstairs though younger.

"Oh, hey there, baby mama."

"Shaw," I say because I'm confused as to why Asher's brother is here. He has his own career, and it isn't in Illinois unless he is on the ice on the opposing team. Asher didn't mention him visiting, either.

He walks right past me. "Tis the holidays, so I thought I would stop on by. Here." His arm darts out to hand me the present.

Pushing the front door, it gingerly closes behind me as I follow Shaw farther into the house, and he looks around, soaking in the setting. "Nice house."

"Oh, I guess you haven't been here since Asher only started this season with the Spinners."

Shaw turns to me with a smile. "Yep. Where is my brother?"

"Here." The sharp tone takes me off guard, and judging by Shaw, he too is experiencing the same. We both look to see Asher slowly walking down the stairs, and he is dressed in dark jeans and a gray sweater, but his hair is still slicked wet. "What a surprise." There is a lack of joy with that sentence.

"Hey, Brother, didn't Mom and Dad tell you that I came to Illinois to visit them since my next game is in Detroit? Then I thought, oh cool, we can drive on out to see my favorite brother."

The dynamic between them feels odd, and maybe it's

because of the age difference or the fact they are on different teams. It could be the reversal of power. Asher is a coach and Shaw still a young player. But right now? Shaw is in the position to succeed at his mission to annoy his brother. A level up from the normal sibling rivalry.

Stepping forward, I want to play mediator because it feels like it might be needed. "Look. He brought a present." I paste on a crooked smile and hold it up, while I give a little shake, only for it to make noises as if it's a rattle.

Shaw glances back at me and grins. "*Yeah*, so the ornament I got kind of broke on the plane, but it's the thought that counts, amiright?"

Asher takes the last step and joins us on the floor. "Gracie, Shaw. Shaw, Gracie," he preambles.

I offer Shaw a polite smile.

"So you're the one making me an uncle." Asher swats the back of his head, and I have to stifle a laugh because they are certainly brothers. "Hey, don't be an ass or I'll tell Mom when they come in." He is totally joking. "They are just grabbing some things from the trunk of the car."

"Nobody in my family decided to text me that you would be early or that you were joining them on their festive ride?" Asher isn't impressed.

"We were too busy with the road trip playlist. This time of year the Maccabeats *Candlelight* song just low key slaps. It's a tune."

I roll my lips in to lock in my laugh. This guy is a character and even Asher manages to soften.

But then reality hits me…

Shit, the entire family are *all* here.

"Okay, totally my cue to go upstairs and change." I'm faster than lightning to escape them. I am not going to stay in Asher's shirt when his parents arrive. Upstairs, I hurry and do my hair and some basic makeup. I drop the world's longest F-bomb when I realize that Asher's eagerness for me to move things in and the fact that I haven't, means I'm down to two options. Cozy long sweater and leggings it is.

Ten minutes later, I'm back downstairs with the sound of voices in the living room. Heading there, lines form on my forehead when I see a fresh poinsettia on the hallway table.

In the living room, Asher's parents instantly beam a smile, and Asher walks to me to relieve me when his arm side-hugs me, calming my nerves that I only now realize that I have.

"There is a poinsettia in the hallway," I mutter to him.

But his mom, Ruby, heard. "My son had the same reaction about the plant." She's completely confused. "I just thought it would give a little cheer and brighten the place up."

"Well, it can certainty brighten a place." Asher's comment makes me chuckle inside. It will be a memory for a lifetime.

He guides me further into the living room, and I don't even get a chance before his mom pulls me into a bear hug that I wasn't expecting. "Look at you with a glow. How are you feeling?"

Pulling away, internally, I rewire to the situation. Casual but peculiar, and crucial for getting to know one another in non-whispering format. "Fine."

Cole, Asher's dad, just gives me a giant smile and touches my shoulder. Okay, I just learned he is not a hugger.

"You're carrying precious goods. The golden grandchild," Shaw mumbles with a full mouth. My eyes whip to him, and he has his feet on the coffee table, making himself at home.

We all sit down with me next to Asher on the sofa. I notice a plate of sufganiyot donuts on the coffee table. I've never seen them on the menu at Jolly Joe's. There are no holes in the middle, instead covered in powder sugar and clearly filled.

Asher notices that I'm checking them out. "These are the ones I told you about. My mom picked some up."

They look damn delicious. "Is that chocolate in one?"

"Praline chocolate. A sort of pudding and my favorite," his dad mentions.

"Well, I'm sold." I lean forward and grab a small plate and opt for a donut with jam to be classic. The moment I take a bite, I'm taken to another galaxy. "Oh my gosh." I continue chewing. It's soft, has a decent amount of strawberry jam filling, and not too sweet.

"If you ever get into an argument with the baby daddy, just get him one of these and you're fine," Shaw suggests so casually.

"How is your team doing this season?" Asher pipes up, clearly taunting his brother because his team is doing terribly.

Their father groans and pinches his nose. "I feel like we just did a time warp and I need to tell my boys to take it down a notch."

Ruby shoos her sons. "Well, here we are. You will be joining the family, Gracie. Anything we should learn about you? I mean, I already know about your career and your parents. How did your parents take the news?"

"Actually, okay."

Asher touches my thigh for a squeeze. "Her dad only thought of killing me for the first few minutes."

"I'm sure. Knocking up his little princess who is younger." Shaw's comment hits a little different this time. A little harsh, perhaps.

I smile tightly at him. "Not an issue. My parents also have an age gap."

Their dad gives Shaw a humorous glare. "Stop it. She's your future sister-in-law."

His words strike me and suddenly the donut falls off my plate because my hands lose balance of holding it straight.

Asher clears his throat because this is not where the conversation was supposed to go. Even though we said that we would go at our own pace and get to know one another, it is all still somehow confronting.

"Wow, really making this a fun day, aren't you," Asher says, sarcastic.

My eyes drop to the blob of dough, red jam, and the cream carpet underneath. "Oh no."

ASHER'S FINGERS cup my elbow. "Don't worry. Stained carpet is the least of our worries right now."

Ruby claps her hands together. "Well, that was a little offside. But I mean, you two are clearly together since she is sleeping here, so that obviously means—"

Asher is quick to interject. "Filter. Use it."

She shrugs her shoulders, but her delightful smile doesn't fade a smidgen. "We are just excited. You sprung a woman and baby on us at the snap of your fingers. It's only been a few days, but here we are on the fifth day of Chrismukkah and we are all in good spirits."

I wipe the corner of my mouth with the back of my finger. "I get it, I do."

Asher shakes his head and blows out a long exhausting breath.

"How is Tyler?" Shaw asks, and I'm relieved that he is changing the subject.

"Fine. He listens well, and we keep it professional," Asher tells him.

"That's good. He is playing better this season," Cole comments then drinks from his mug of coffee.

There is a moment of silence, and it is kind of awkward, but we all look at one another and acknowledge it. "Uh…"

"Baby shower," Ruby throws out a topic.

"Right. I mean, it's early, so all of that is for later. I know my mom wants one."

She pulls her dark hair to the side. "Of course."

"Probably at Olive Owl. My brother and his wife's family, as you know, are there. They are all a little angry that one of the nieces didn't have her baby shower there, so I'm being used to compensate for that." It is a great place for a party.

"Love it. It will be so cute when the baby comes and you have those little headphones for when she or he comes to a game when you're sitting with the other WAGs." She winks at Asher.

"Oh hell," he utters to himself.

My lips roll into my mouth as I bite my lip to keep myself in check. She's eager for a label but all in lighthearted spirit.

"I really am loving this morning. Pure entertainment. And Gracie, if you can handle this, then you will be fine. So, welcome to the family," Shaw compliments before grabbing another donut.

The squeeze of my arm brings my attention to Asher whose eyes are warm and reassuring.

The next two hours, we eat quiche and bagels, talk about my work and Ruby's photography. There isn't much discussion about the baby or the status of our relationship, and everything flows. When they leave, we hug goodbye, and Shaw gives me an honest grin.

Asher closes the door behind him, and his entire body eases with relief.

"Well, we've survived your family and mine."

"We did. It seems all is well." I plant my hands on my belly and look down with only affection. "You will be very loved, little one."

"She or he will." His voice is soft, and when I draw my gaze up, I see that his stare is locked on my belly.

"Family, huh?"

"Yep. Family."

Because we are creating our own.

# CHAPTER 14
## ASHER

A smile twists on Gracie's lips as I sit at her kitchen island and observe her and the joy that seems to be flooding her face. It was my first day back with the team since the short break, and I have a time gap after our morning practice. So I came home and presented Gracie with a small gift.

"Well played, well played." She holds up her fluffy pair of mint-green wool socks that will keep her feet and calves warm throughout winter. The snowflake design is a nice touch, if I do say so myself.

"I just figured it's important that you are cozy. Plus, Hanukkah tradition and all."

"Socks," we both say in unison.

She tucks the socks back into the gift bag and sets it on the counter. A beaming smile spreads on her beautiful face. "Tradition seems to be us… well, half of the time." She drops her eyes to her stomach with a brief cartoonish expression before returning to her smile.

"Whoa, according to our parents, he or she is a Hanukkah

miracle. Having one of those every holiday season is tradition."

She chuffs a laugh as she circles the island. "*Yeah*, as much as my dad is happy about a new grandchild, he will *always* let you know that we skipped the marriage-first part."

Blowing out a breath, I'm well aware she is right. I notice that she grabs a little gift bag that was hidden behind the fruit bowl.

"What's that?" I wonder.

"Well, great minds think alike." She approaches me, grinning like a Cheshire cat, then extends her arm to offer me the bag. "Cheesy Hanukkah gifts. Except, I think yours has more class."

I'm already grinning as I tuck my hand into the bag only to feel soft fabric, and I pull out the pair of dark socks. "Should I be concerned that we never even talked about gifts, yet here we are surprising one another?"

She laughs and walks straight to me, resting her arm on my shoulder for a side embrace as she stares at the socks. "No, concerned should be that I went the extra step on silly gifts."

Giving the socks a once-over, I chuckle. "Hot dad." It's the pattern of words on the socks.

"I couldn't help myself. It was that or the tie. But I figured you could wear these with your suit and nobody would know."

I side-eye her. "That's a well-thought plan."

She interlaces her hands together. "I know. I'm such a smart cookie, except on the birth control front," she gushes.

"Let's test that." I pat her behind and stand, giving her a light little shove in the direction of her bedroom, and I trail behind. "How is the packing going? I can help with the heavy things."

"Swell." She doesn't sound enthusiastic.

I instantly touch her arm to force her eyes in my direction. "You're okay with this, right? I mean the moving-in part. You don't sound thrilled, and if it's too much then just say so."

Gracie shakes her head once and rolls her lips in, with her eyes having a hint of concern. "It's not that at all. I'm completely okay with moving in." The sincerity is strong. "It's just…"

She groans then yanks my arm and tows me along straight to her room. The moment I step foot in the room, I know why she didn't seem thrilled by my packing inspection.

A large empty box rests in the middle of the room on a rug.

"I'm not so good at packing," she explains. "Even more so when I won't even fit into most of these clothes in the coming months. That is confronting, and I'm kind of… well… scared I will just be resorting to ugly maternity dresses or something, then I will just be fat and unattractive. It's the first spring that I won't be able to wear my vintage flower dress that fits me to a T," she squeaks out.

I do my best to bury the laugh because she's being ridiculous, and I believe she's aware of it too.

It's two steps to her, and I capture her wrist, turning her until her back is to my front and we are both staring directly at the full-length mirror.

"I very much disagree on all of that." I inch the fabric of her shirt up until it's bunched at the band of her bra. Then I place the palms of my hands around her still-flat belly. "See this?"

She nods.

I bring her close to me, our bodies enfolded. "Our baby is in there. It's so fucking sexy that you're carrying my child."

Her brows shoot up and now a smile ghosts on her mouth. "*Your* child?"

"Our child," I correct myself, even though the internal caveman in me enjoys saying my child. Nuzzling my nose into that sensitive spot by her ear, I murmur against her hair. "You're beautiful, and as this baby grows inside of you, you will glow even more."

She studies herself in the mirror, my hands staying put on her belly. "Your mom told me that you were a big baby," she deadpans.

My teeth capture her ear for a gentle touch. "Everyone will see what I did to you," I whisper.

Our eyes meet in the mirror, and I see how she is now convinced, and I kiss her neck in satisfaction that I made my point. She turns her head and offers me her lips, and I give her what she seeks. I brush her lips with mine, nuzzling our noses, and she chases after my mouth, but I enjoy this dance with her.

But it doesn't take long for her to win. Our firm kiss is a confirmation. We're at a good place, she and I. Her body twists until she's square with me, and she drapes her arms over my shoulders.

"Care to take this to bed?" she hums.

Tempting. So very tempting.

"Not yet. I only reward good behavior. So why don't you do something with the box."

She frowns and shoves my shoulder. "Mood killer."

I chuckle, and we step away from one another. Her hand finds her chin while she contemplates. "Okay, clothes I won't fit into."

"Lies."

"Shoes that need a lot of space."

"Knew that was coming," I volley back.

Her hand plops down at her side, and she looks at me, puzzled. "We haven't really discussed past romantic entanglements. Have you ever lived with a woman?"

Yikes. My jaw ticks, and I attempt a nervous smile. "Not relevant."

"So that's a yes?"

"Many, many years ago. I'm older than you, remember?" I answer simply.

Her chin slides side to side, and her nails tap against her hips. "Huh… okay. Well, her loss is my gain… unless it didn't work because you never put your dishes in the dishwasher? Could be a dealbreaker."

I'm relieved she is taking this conversation in stride.

"No worries there." My smile is dampened.

She points her finger at me. "Well, I'm sure she didn't provide you with both Hanukkah and festive cheer. That reminds me, I have a Hanukkah ornament for the Christmas tree that you failed to have. My grandmother gave it to me for my first Chrismukkah. Don't you worry, my father doesn't think that item is cursed." She walks on by me and pats my shoulder. "That year, anyhow."

"Fine. We'll store it next to my elf figure for next year," I mention seriously.

Gracie stops in her tracks and turns on her heel. She seems shocked. "You have one of those stuffed elf dolls?"

I lift my shoulders as if it's nothing. "Did I not mention that? Oops, my bad."

"You, Asher Tate, Mr. Badass Hockey Coach, have an elf that kids believe comes alive at night and sits on shelves?"

Licking my lips, I smile until my cheeks hurt. "Relax. It's in a closet somewhere… and let's not call it a doll. It's an action figure. I'm surprised my mom didn't tell you. Shaw has the Hanukkah version."

She excitedly claps her hands together. "This is great. Next year we can do it with the baby."

Now I just need to shut her down. "Uh, he or she won't even be crawling yet."

"Okay, maybe it will be more for me," she admits.

"Topic closed. Shall we pack a little?" I urge us along.

She throws her hands into the air and huffs. "I guess I start with shoes."

Gracie steps toward her closet, but I reach for her wrist and reel her in to me. "Hey." My voice grows tender the moment I feel the electric spark when I touch her. "I have a feeling living with you will be an adventure and a good kind."

She lifts her nose and has a wistful look. "Asher… I think so too."

And she nuzzles herself into my arms as I wrap her close.

Until now, I always assumed luck would lead to a winning game. But I'm not playing any games with Gracie. I'm lucky because I met her, and now we are growing to know one another, well aware we will have a lifetime together.

# CHAPTER 15
## GRACIE

I'm waiting for my best friend to say something because I just told her the big news. Although, I feel guilty for not telling her sooner, I knew she would understand. I sit cozily on her couch while I watch her reaction, which is somewhat amusing.

"P-Pregnant?" She's definitely in shock.

"That I am." I'm completely relaxed and feel my smile wanting to break out as I play it casual.

"And with the coach?" She's still in disbelief, it seems.

I nod in confirmation.

"As in you and he are going to be parents."

Staring at her blankly, I wonder how long we will go in circles. "You heard me the first time."

She touches my knee. "How?"

"One of those annoying October storms of rain and sleet, finding shelter, and chewing on candy, you know how it goes. Then boom, a few weeks later, you learn a baby is on the way. A complete Chrismukkah miracle, right?"

"Who else knows?"

"Our parents." As much as I want to go into every detail,

I want to discuss her current situation. I refuse to make this whole conversation about me. "You know what? Let's leave the baby talk for another time. I need a distraction, so can we talk about something else?"

"Sure. Just know that I'm here for you, and if you're happy then so am I," she assures me, and she means every word.

"Thanks, but you are also happy because of a certain hockey player," I point out.

Lainey's blush says it all. She's completely falling for the guy she always thought she hated.

"You were watching the locker-room interviews after his game when I arrived." There is no way I'm not calling her out on that.

And for the next twenty minutes we discuss her accidental Chrismukkah day with his family and the fact they have slept together. Tis the season. Being with Asher lately in bed, it's different to our first night that created a baby; better.

Lainey waves her hand in front of my face. "Yoo-hoo. Earth to baby mama."

My eyes pop out as I stall in my transport from daydreaming and re-enter the current world. "Yes?"

"I could have told you that I murdered someone and hid the body with clues for you to find to help the police, and you would have no idea."

Shrugging a shoulder, I must admit defeat. "Okay, maybe I do need to get this whole pregnancy with the hot coach thing off my chest."

Lainey throws her hands in the air. "Finally."

I brush her up on my excitement, how our parents found out, and Asher's demand that I move in with him. It's just the one piece that I have no answer to when Lainey tries to break down what I'm feeling.

Leaning against the sofa with my feet tucked under my legs, I hold my cup of tea between my hands. "I'd be crazy not to contemplate the future. I curse schedules and biology for making me tired. New Year's Eve the team is playing an afternoon away game, but they probably won't be back early enough."

Lainey is looking like a complete smartass right now, filled with glee as she both teases me and is eager to break me down. "You love New Year's which means perfect timing for puzzle pieces to fit together and become more logical with one another about what is happening between you two. I can see it on your face that for anyone to be the dad, then you are very happy that it's him."

Smiling to myself, I'm aware every word she says is true. "How can I not be? I mean, maybe we had a few questionable moments, such as saying we would be only one time, or some words were not well chosen when we found out, but he is stepping up. We didn't know one another well at all, but now we learn more every day, and it feels right. Not only that, but I want to fuck him into next Chrismukkah. That's a bonus."

She chuffs a laugh. "Attraction is a bonus if you are both going to try. That's what you are doing, right?"

"Being together? I mean, maybe we haven't said it specifically, but everything we do leads that way."

"Well, that's promising."

Searching for my sweater that I threw on the arm of the sofa, I feel confident too. "It is." I slide on my cardigan as I stand. "I'm sorry, but I'm going to get going. There are just a few errands I need to run, and I know your son will last only so long on his tablet in his room."

"So true." She hops up to accompany me back to the front door, then we stop to give our usual hug goodbye. "Just give it all a chance. I think you two will be fine, and I love that for you."

I give her a knowing look. "Someone should take their own advice."

"Get out of here." She grins.

WE DIDN'T THINK this through. Am I just supposed to make space in the bathroom drawer for my things?

I'm at Asher's house and figured I should unpack a few more things. He's been bugging me that I haven't been bringing over enough suitcases. His flight should be landing soon, which means I'm alone here to fend for myself. But without direction, I'm trying to skirt around boundaries.

"Meh." I shrug and claim a drawer on the right. He'll have to get used to my boldness. Swooping up all of his hotel shampoos, I throw them to the ground; I'll sort it out later. I place my things in the drawer that I've now claimed.

Whether he minds or not, I've come to realize that he is used to my quirks, and he hasn't complained once. That's a good sign for two people who maybe could be more than just parents together.

After ruffling through another drawer in his bedroom, I decide it's time to conquer the living room.

A quick power snack and drink and I'm unpacking a bag of gold-and-silver garland that I bought. Post-Christmas means decorations are 60% off at the store, and that's a win. The fireplace mantel is the only spot that doesn't require tape or me standing on a ladder.

Just as I'm making the final touches of the gold wrapped with silver on the edge of the mantel, I hear the door open, and my heart lifts. It's excitement.

"Hey, I'm he—" Asher is still in his suit when he stops in his tracks as he enters the living room, and he stares blankly at the fireplace. "What the hell is that?"

"Ta-da." My hands display the garland. "A little sparkle for New Year's. It was a little dull around here, and I love New Year's Eve. You can get mega excited because I also got hats and noisemakers."

The way he tuts at me is far sexier than I think he intends. "Not a fan of your glittery decorations."

I fake a frown and silently laugh as he begins to loosen his collar.

"Don't." It comes out a little eager from my end.

He stops before he begins to undo a button. I'm well aware that when I stride to him that my hips sway. I'm not sure he notices, as his eyes are fixed with mine. Arriving to him, I fist his shirt and step closer, causing our bodies to be flush.

"You look good in a suit."

"And you look good with clothes on the floor." His voice today is deeper and dripping with sin while his hands square my hips as he pulls me tighter to his body.

He's a wall of warmth and firmness, and it feels secure and stable, and it isn't just a physical thing.

The way his eyes dip down and focus on my mouth, it's clear that there is a hunger in his body, and I'm what is on the menu. It's only confirmed as he walks me backwards, with merely a deep hum leaving his lips. The entire journey to his room he keeps me captive purely with his eyes.

He's determined to get my clothes on the floor, that's for sure.

When the backs of my knees hit the end of the mattress, I flop down to sitting as he towers over me, and he loosens the cuffs of his sleeves. I should probably be stripping down to the lace on my body, but my eyes are glued to him. Just because I don't look away doesn't mean I can't assist with unbuckling his pants. But my hands don't get far because as soon as they touch the buckle, Asher pushes me to my back and lies next to me on his side.

Suddenly, the passionate need seems to simmer down.

"If you dragged me here only to sleep, then I need to tell you that sleeping in your bed is literally not happening," I quip quietly.

His long finger lands on my mouth to shush me. "Want to know something?" I nod. "You've invaded my thoughts. After the game when my mind should shoot all focus toward how to improve for the next game, they went straight to you. Your laugh, your beautiful smile, the way you can be unpredictable, your lips that taste of peaches, and the fact that being away from you does things to me."

"What might that be?" I whisper against his lips, entranced because it seems that we are on the same page.

"It seems I miss you and hate that I haven't been able to keep you in my bed every night and keep you warm. The whole flight I felt heavy, and maybe that can only be described as excitement because I want you."

Shifting to my side, I touch his face with my hand because this moment is a big step. "I should be worried that we are only feeling this because we are blinded by a baby that binds us, but it's not that at all, is it?"

His hand follows the curve of my body up then ends with his thumb pressing against my bottom lip. "It's not. We seem to be right for one another. You actually make me a little less uptight, and that's pure mystical powers that only you seem to have."

I glance away, only for Asher to guide my chin and gaze back to him. "I'm not going to deny nor debate your observation. You and I have eased into one another, two strong-willed people, and that can backfire for some, but… I don't think it will for us. I don't want to ignore it."

His face is filled with the tenacity that he is known for. "We're not going to. I'm not sure this is us even trying to be something. We just walked right into us, and we don't even need to try."

I feel like I'm glowing as bliss fills my lungs. "I want this." My conviction is strong as a vow.

"Me too."

He brushes his lips over mine, almost shy, afraid to break a spell between us. But finally, he kisses me with firmness, unhurried.

The feeling of his palms cupping my face makes it feel as though he will hold us together and not in a physical sense. When we create space, his eyes have a gleam of affection, and gosh, I'm lucky.

Is he disapproving?

Asher is sitting on the floor next to the fireplace that he turned on with a switch. "Really? You have to walk in like that?"

I give my body the once-over and proudly grin. "You just had me naked in your bed, and you are scared of a little lingerie?" I'm wearing a silver lace bra and panties with an open lace robe.

"I'm going to have to get used to this, aren't I?" He doesn't sound disappointed about that.

I join him on the floor and grab a nearby throw blanket because it is a little nippy in here. "Perks of having the woman in your bed be part of a lingerie dynasty."

He adjusts the blanket on my body. "There are worse things. Just don't want you to get cold right now."

I appreciate that, but I'm getting distracted. "Ooh, snacks." I spot the plate on the fireplace ledge and reach to pick up the plate of crackers and cookies. My body length falls short, and Asher is my hero to help and offers me the plate.

"I wasn't sure what the baby feels like eating today."

Biting into the cookie, my tastebuds approve. "I'm not sure, but want to know something amazing about the new year?"

He scoots closer to me and grabs a cracker. "Enlighten me."

"I can eat as many cookies as I want until the summer, and nobody will bat an eyelash because I'll be fat anyways."

"I'm pretty sure that a positive pregnancy doesn't make you fat." He looks over his shoulder at the bottle of champagne on the table. "Don't worry, it's sparkling grape juice."

"Didn't want to do the party hats?" I'm flippant, and his blank face is his answer. "I'll take that as a no."

He quickly checks the time on his watch. "Since we got distracted in my bed, it's already twenty minutes to midnight."

I interlink our arms and cuddle into him. "Well then, it seems we are playing a few rounds of twenty questions."

He kisses the top of my head. "I'm only doing this game for you."

Perfect answer.

He already treats me like a queen, and I'm confident to say that I deserve to be treated that way, just like he deserves my all. For the next few minutes, we learn more about each other. No topics off the table. His hidden talent for playing piano, my fear of corn mazes. The demands of his career and the creative process for mine. We're both on board for finding out if the baby is a boy or girl. If it wasn't for my yawn and him checking the time, then we would almost miss the clock at midnight.

Popping the cork, he pours juice into two flutes then hands me one.

"Not going to lie. I would be in bed sleeping if it wasn't for you."

"Old man."

"Call me that again and I have no problem establishing punishment in this place."

Have I stopped smiling? No, not once.

"Challenging me isn't a smart move. It makes me want to do it even more."

"I know." His gives me a knowing look that sends a sensation straight to my pussy.

He clinks our glasses. "To a new year with new beginnings and welcoming a healthy kid who will turn our world upside down."

"Couldn't have said it better myself." We both take a sip, only for me to spit out the juice while Asher begins to retch, and our faces sour. "Eww. What is this?"

"I had a bottle along with the other wines." Lifting the bottle, he studies the label. "Sorry it's not your Blisswood wine that your dad has an abundance of." His face looks revolted from what we just swallowed. "Oh no. I started the year with making my pregnant girlfriend sick." His eyes slide up to meet mine. "It's wine from Passover. My mom hates the red wine at Passover, and my dad prefers white at Easter."

"And? What does that have to do with this awful taste?" I wipe the back of my hand over the corner of my mouth.

He sets the bottle down. "It seems... the year on the bottle... well, it's from Passover three years ago."

"Who the hell keeps grape juice three years old?" I squeak.

"The guy who is too distracted by the woman prancing around his house in lingerie."

I pull him closer to me by squeezing his arm. "I've already warned you to get used to it. Now, please clean out that collection of yours and pass me a cracker to soak up that mishap."

He titters in response before affectionately kissing my forehead.

"You're going to have to do a lot more than a chaste kiss." I pretend to be in a foul mood.

"Of course." He begins to move and rises up on his knees in front of me, then he slowly peels the blanket off my body. "How about I tell you happy New Year then worship every little inch of you."

"I mean, not exactly a *bad* way to start the year." I give up on my theatrics and pull on his hands. "Happy New Year, now come here."

"*Yeah*, not going to take you here on the floor. My plan was a few kisses, maybe nipple sucking, then carry you to my room. You're pregnant. You deserve a soft mattress."

What a Prince Charming.

"Then get me there now."

Yep. Best New Year's yet.

# CHAPTER 16
## ASHER

Glancing at my watch as I stand between the bench and ice, I'm well aware that I'm going to play nice and let the team go early from practice. They've earned it after our win, but our best forward is on a game-to-game decision, as he was cleared to play after an upper-body injury, but I'm not convinced he is ready for the ice. I've had to call up someone from the minors, and that line needs to practice.

But really, why am I going to end this practice early? Logistics. I need to get to Gracie's doctor's appointment. Missing the last one was not what I wanted, but this is the life we have to juggle during hockey season.

With Gracie settled now at my place, I was quick to notice a few things. She never said it, but I know that she was disappointed that I missed the last appointment. Sometimes she hides behind the excuse that she understands because it is what her mom experienced when her dad was coaching. I do believe her, but deep down, I know she wishes that in this moment it was different. The only thing I'm confident about is that she constantly reiterates that her childhood was amazing, even if her dad's schedule was not ideal, and it will be the same for our child.

I'm trying my best, and no matter what, I'll be there today. I *want* to be there.

Checking the goalies who are busy doing drills with the goaltending coach, I scan my vision back to our captain who is discussing a few techniques with our call-up. None of us are blind; when you are making your major league debut, then you have nerves.

"Asher, do you want to go over the video of Tampa?" My assistant coach hands me a tablet, as he's been busy analyzing who we are playing next.

"Sure, but I'm going to have to run in ten." The smile playing on my lips that I'm trying to hide is a fail.

The secret is slowly spilling out. At my meeting the other day with our GM, I had to break the news because if the baby comes early, then the date comes right smack dab around the draft in June. While Vaughn Madden, who has been our GM for years, didn't seem to make a big deal about it, I'm not sure he would show how he has to change some piece of the puzzle in June. He's always valued input from the head coach, and it's my first year with the team. Yet, guilt didn't cross my mind, not even once.

For a baby that was completely unexpected, I'm feeling how she or he is a game changer in my life, Gracie too. She is the perfect one to scare any of my stress away, and I look forward to returning home every single time.

Over my assistant coach's shoulder, I see Declan appear and stand by the entrance. He crosses his arms and lifts his chin in a nod, suggesting that I should join him.

I hand the tablet back. "Sorry. Just give me a moment."

Walking to Declan, his tiny smile should be disconcerting

to some, but not me. I have a hunch about what this conversation is going to be.

"Congratulations," he tells me.

A smirk tilts on my mouth. "I figured that Vaughn would tell you."

Declan tips his head to the side. "We're a family, this team, so good news spreads fast. But actually, it was the grandfather-to-be. He burst out his excitement over a scotch last night at dinner."

We asked them to wait, but it was useless because Gracie herself let it slip the other day when she was fitting one of her mother's friends at the boutique.

My droll smile is mixed with amusement. "You told me to keep sponsors happy," I joke.

Declan slaps his hand on my shoulder, grinning. "Well, Hudson sure as hell isn't going to stop sponsorship if his future son-in-law is the coach. Might even be in our favor. It also means that we can never fire you."

We both chuckle. Although funny, there may be some deep truth to that.

"He's just a sponsor. It's not like he is the team owner and his daughter is with the new guy on the team." Why did that fly out of me? It's in a moment of laughter, and I wasn't thinking.

Declan stills, and his jaw tightens. "What did you just say?"

"Nothing. A bad joke." And probably covering my ass because even I fear one day it might be a reality that we all have to face.

Declan swings his gaze to the ice and locks on the player just traded to our team, the one with not the greatest reputation. Then slowly his steely look returns to me. His fear is replaced by a bright fake smile. "Theoretically, right? Anyhow, did Vaughn also talk to you about potential trades?"

Inhaling a deep breath, I hate this predicament that I might find myself in. "He is the GM, I'm the coach. If you want to trade for my brother, then that is your prerogative. He will be just a player to me. Just like Tyler is."

Declan crosses his arms. "Okay. Just checking. You will obviously keep this under wraps."

"No need to say that." I can't discuss this with my brother because then it really can mess up any future team changes.

"Well, congratulations again."

"Thanks. I've got to get going, Gracie has a doctor's appointment. The coaching staff can handle the guys." I hike my thumb behind me.

Declan whistles in concern. "Might want to leave ASAP. The snow that started an hour ago is really coming down. I'm actually surprised nobody from the front office told you guys. If it holds up like they say it will, then there will be problems with flights later."

"Shit." My only issue with that sentence is that I'll miss the appointment. "Off I go then."

I trot back to the bench to grab my coat. While I'm swinging on my coat, Tyler brakes on his skates in front of me on the other side of the bench.

He carefully looks around because the team, including myself if I'm honest, sometimes forget that we are related. "Congratulations." My eyes bug out, waiting for an answer to a question he already knows as I zip up. "Both our parents were at dinner at our aunt's house." His face turns lopsided.

"How bad?"

"Like five minutes in, probably. I don't think anybody needed alcohol to let the news get out." Of course, it's not only Gracie's family failing on the keeping-it-cool level.

Quickly glancing at my watch, I feel the urgency. "Sounds about right. Thanks, though. I'm leaving for an appointment, so there will probably only be a few more drills before you guys can go. Apparently, the snow is coming down outside."

He skates off, and I nearly run out. The moment I open the door from the rink, I feel screwed.

The fresh level of snow is soft, but there is a layer on the road as more flakes fall. I make it to the car and start the engine to warm up, and I grab my scraper to push snow off the windows. The moment I'm back in my car, I call Gracie on the Bluetooth.

She picks up instantly. "Hey, everything okay? I'm here."

"Here? The appointment isn't for another twenty minutes."

"But I like to be on time, and the roads meant driving slower." I'm thankful, in a way, because she is in the waiting room and no longer on the road driving where it is too dangerous.

Carefully, I drive out of the parking lot with the realization that I won't be topping twenty miles on the road. There is no way that I'll make it on time.

"I'm in the car, but I doubt I'll be there in twenty."

"*Oh.*"

She is 100% disheartened.

"I'm going to try. Maybe ask if they can wait?"

"Asher," she grumbles. "We're not royalty, and there are other people with an appointment, too."

I'm careful as I turn but still my car swerves slightly. "I'm doing my best. I don't want to miss this." I'm already furious at mother nature.

"I hope not." Oh fuck, she sounds miserable and sad. This is the worst-case scenario because we've been talking about the appointment all week. She even booked it knowing it wasn't a game day.

All I can do is beg for a miracle and hope the local property taxes here means there is a goddamn snowplow doing its job right now.

ALREADY I'M fifteen minutes late, and I'm running on adrenaline. This can't be happening. I can't bear to miss this. Not only to be there for Gracie but also the baby. They are a package deal. I'm also curious, as I haven't been to an appointment.

The doctor's office is on the other side of the red light at the intersection, but I'm relying on the three cars in front of me to drive ahead. If I thought I was going at a snail's pace, then I can safely say that they are even slower. In the end, they too need to be safe.

It feels like forever before I manage to reach the parking lot, but then I need to search for a spot because there are few and my car is too big. Finally, I succeed, but running to the entrance isn't an option, as the snow is also icy.

This all feels like another power is testing me.

Even when I make it through the sliding doors and straight to reception, I still feel that the finish line isn't here yet.

Reaching the desk almost panting, which says a lot because I'm fit, means this is a crisis taking its toll both mentally and physically. "I'm here for an appointment for Gracie Arrows." I'm out of breath, and the young receptionist in a uniform stares at me impassively.

"Right. The husband."

"Yes." I don't feel the need to correct her. And wait, did Gracie call me that?

"She's already in, but you can go down the hall to the second door on the right."

Running straight ahead, I don't care that I burst the door to the examination room open to find Gracie is already lying on the examination table with the doctor preparing a few items.

Gracie smiles brightly when she sees me.

"Did I miss it?" I finally ease.

She holds out her hand, inviting me to join her. "You're just on time. We were in luck and the woman before us took longer than planned."

Blowing out a sigh of relief, I run my hands through my hair. "Thank fuck."

The doctor pauses and looks at me, probably due to my choice of words, but she smirks to herself. "Believe it or not, you are not the first to be late. Now, pull up a chair and we'll get started."

I spot the small wheely stool and slide it to be closer to Gracie who is already lifting her shirt up to reveal her tiny bump. I can't help noticing her bra choice today, and she most definitely gets points for her choice of blue lace.

"You made it," she whispers and scoots a little to find a better position.

"Okay, we're going to get started," the doctor announces. "I was just saying to Gracie that if someone plays nice in the belly, then we might be able to discover if the baby is a boy or girl, unless you don't want to know."

"We want to know," Gracie and I say in unison.

The doctor grins. "Clear. I'm going to do a few measurements on the screen first."

She starts pressing buttons on her screen in unison with

moving the wand on the now-visible slope of Gracie's belly. I just focus on Gracie who stares at me in marvel. Maybe it's because I made it or that she knows what is about to happen. Either way, I can't help but smile.

The sound of the baby's heartbeat floods the room, and I can't help but be affected. It's fast, strong, and I helped create it. This isn't the same as listening on my phone from the last video. Now, I'm here in real time, and the baby looks bigger, a clear outline of head and legs, with beating heart in the middle.

"Wow, this is…" A long breath leaves me as I try to figure out what this feeling and emotion is.

Gracie tugs on my hand. "Crazy." She admires the screen, too.

"Nausea subsiding?" the doctor asks.

"Yes," Gracie answers.

"Sleep?"

"Still a little more than normal."

"Taking your vitamins?"

"Another yes."

The doctor looks up from the wand on Gracie's stomach to check her screen. "Everything is looking healthy on this end. Growing well and nothing unusual."

Gracie and I couldn't erase the smiles on our faces if we tried.

"*And* I most definitely can tell you that someone is cooperating with us today." The doctor seems just as excited as us.

I swoop Gracie's hand into mine and kiss the back of it, keeping our fingers interlaced. "Not going to lie, I'm finding this all surreal," I admit, with the swimming of exhilaration inside me.

"I just can't believe that this baby is inside my body."

"Ready?" the doctor checks.

For a moment, the whole room seems to hold their breath in anticipation.

She points with her finger to the area on the screen that I quickly attempt to study. "Congratulations on your little girl."

Suddenly, everything feels real.

Gracie covers her mouth as she smiles, and a joyful tear drizzles down her cheek.

"A girl," I whisper and kiss her forehead. "A daughter."

Holy fuck, I'm outnumbered. I already feel wrapped around my daughter's little finger, and she isn't even out of the womb.

Gracie begins to rumble a chuckle as she rests her head back. "This also means that we are saved."

We both would have been happy with whatever, but there is one thing that we don't need to worry about. Gracie turns her head while she rests against the exam bed and our eyes meet. We are on the same wavelength.

"Oh, thank goodness. No more circumcision talk from your family and your great-grandmother haunting us."

We both burst out laughing, and I lean down to give her a peck on her lips before trailing my mouth near her ear to whisper so only she can hear. "Nice choice of lace today, by the way." I noticed her panty choice as soon as I came in, with her pants waistband pulled lower. Pulling away, she must notice the hunger that seeped through every word of that sentence.

"Always."

"Alright, let's go over a few more things, then you can get out of here. I think the snow will only get worse," the doctor notes.

"Don't worry. I won't be letting Gracie drive, so we will have to pick up her car tomorrow," I assure the room.

Gracie rolls her eyes because she knows that I'm in protective mode.

"Good plan." The doctor ties the appointment up in the next few minutes. "Just make another appointment and then we are good to go."

"Yep." Gracie slides on her coat.

Following Gracie to reception, I can't seem to let my hand fall from the small of her back. She begins to talk to the lady behind the desk, and I look around the now-vacant waiting room and notice the heavy snow outside.

Gracie grabs my attention with her hand touching my shoulder. "Maybe you can come then? It's the season bye week. Is there a day that could work?"

"I'll still have a lot of strategy meeting with the coaching staff. But let's do a Tuesday that week and then I'll check."

The receptionist types into the computer then smiles at us. "A Valentine's Day appointment. Love those."

My head perks up from her reminder.

Valentine's Day.

I hate it.

Chocolates, hearts, teddy bears, and roses that will die within a week.

Yet, my mind is already formulating ideas to make the woman next to me happy.

Maybe chocolate hearts aren't so bad. They can have caramel in them, right? Or even better, I can just lay them in a row on her body to eat my way up to her tits that are growing.

Suddenly, I'm freaking excited for Valentine's Day.

# CHAPTER 17
## GRACIE

Popping a chocolate into my mouth, I moan from the taste of praline cream. The box on the counter at the boutique arrived perfectly wrapped, which has now been half destroyed. I have a knack for ignoring the guide of what each chocolate is and instead opt for biting into each one until I find a favorite.

I'll give a point to Asher because I wasn't expecting this. I just kind of figured he hates Valentine's Day. In fact, I can imagine him grumbling at every red item at the grocery store. I bet he was not impressed when team marketing took photos of the players holding roses and stuffed bears.

Still nibbling on my chocolate, I see my mom proudly holding up a hanger with a maroon satin bra and a matching cover-up that has a slit that would fall along the valley between breasts. She gawks her eyes at me while I continue to casually nosh on my treat.

"It's great for Valentine's Day and perfect so you don't need to worry about your growing belly."

Her conviction causes me to stall mid-chew. "Are you serious right now?" We're quite open with one another, one major reason for why women shop here. Still… "Can we end this conversation now?"

She sets her choice of apparel on a nearby railing. "What? I'm just trying to help. It's not like you two are just co-parenting. There is a little more to that. I'm not blind, you two are sharing a bed."

I cringe, absolutely cringe. "Geez, crossing boundaries." My spine straightens, and I hold my palm up to stop her.

My mom gives me a knowing look. "Fine. I'm just presenting options should you choose to use them." She crosses her arms and almost huffs. "The color really makes your eyes pop."

I slowly shake my head. "Conversation ended ten seconds ago," I warn her.

Undeniably, this is kind of funny, but also a little awkward.

"Okay, but you two are together, and it seems to be going well. What are your plans for today?"

I shrug a shoulder as I pick up a ribbon that I was using before to pair with a design I'm creating for a very appropriate, lines-not-crossed, spring dress. "Nothing. A box of chocolates is fine."

My mom seems very unimpressed. "Even if a man hates the holiday, they will love it if you make them love it. Galentine's day is fun and all, but now you have the man to give you the real thing. Just give him a little push."

I roll my eyes at her. "Let me guess. Lingerie," I deadpan.

She pretends to swipe something off the sleeve of her shirt. "If you think it's a good idea, I have options."

When I was younger, I felt as though my mom was a bit more reserved, but with age, she has become more outspoken. Right now proves that fact.

The sound of the bell ringing over the door brings our

attention to Lainey who just entered. "Hi, ladies." She sounds cheery today.

"Good to see you. What brings you in today?" My mom smiles.

"Something new. I actually hate this holiday, and I'm sure Tyler will think it's a normal day, but I kind of feel like reminding him later, and maybe he'll feel a little guilty and then he is more eager to agree next time I request something." She smiles and is already eyeing a nightie number on the wall. "Wearing his jersey only gets me so far."

My mom seems to be in her glory right now. "See, daughter of mine. A smart move by your best friend."

Ignoring them both, I search for another chocolate to be my next victim.

"Ooh, chocolates." Lainey walks over and helps herself to one. "I love these. It's great how everyone on the team found the same gift to send."

I stop in the middle of my bite, drop the sweet in one thud, and draw my eyes up to my friend. "What?" My tone is sharp.

"Yeah. Apparently, it's some tradition that all the guys send their other half the same chocolates. Least they remember it's Valentine's Day, right? Actually, it's the marketing department sending on their behalf." She searches for a chocolate that she must already be familiar with.

"Oh," I let out blandly.

Lainey looks at me, slightly worried. "You okay? If it's any consolation, my expectations for my first Valentine's Day with Tyler are low because I told him many times how much I hate this day. Lingerie will throw him off, though."

My mother presses her lips together to lock in her approving laugh, only to swallow and touch my friend's shoulder. "A wonderful idea. See anything you like? The maroon number might be reserved for my stubborn daughter," she says as if it's a normal conversation.

Lainey abandons her chocolate and steps to the nearby display. "Ooh, that's gorgeous, but I think I will stick with the purple one I have my eye on."

They both look at me.

I hold in my breath only to huff it out in a groan and my arm darts out. "Fine. Give me the outfit."

Maybe Lainey is right, and we should remind our significant others what day it is.

MY HANDS ADJUST my straps as I stand in the middle of the living room with a silk robe on. Appraising the lit candles, I'm satisfied. Even on a normal night, I cozy up with candles. Lately it's been fleece pajamas and the TV on to watch the away games. Tonight, I'm going back to my roots.

My eyes sink down to my belly, and my hand naturally finds home there. "I mean, technically, your dad sees me like this all the time. Which, by the way, if your grandmother wishes to discuss the family company, then run... far away. It's okay if your dad doesn't remember what today is, everything else feels perfect anyhow."

I quirk my lips out and check the clock on the wall. Asher should be home any moment, and now they are off for the week. The players are, anyway, Asher not so much.

The moment I hear the door open, I feel my heart skip. Why am I nervous?

Suddenly, it hits me why. The man I'm having a child with is actually the man that I love, really love. Maybe we've both been falling fast, but we haven't stopped for a long moment to really say it.

"Gracie, I'm home. Want me to start the fireplaaaa… whoa." He stills when he enters the living room, and he seems to drink up the view.

My brows furrow, because I wasn't expecting him to be carrying a bunch of roses that are the color of what I'm wearing, nor was I expecting a small gift bag and a box from the bakery in town.

"Did you only remember the holiday because the team sends chocolates?" I'm skeptical as he places his gifts down on the sofa in passing.

He slowly walks my way as if he is hunting and I'm his prey. "Actually, I had it circled in my calendar, with not only one but three reminders popping up over the last few days." His hands encircle my wrists.

"Really?" I'm in doubt. "I kind of thought you must hate this day."

"Oh, I do, but I'm falling in love with you, so now I like this day. Flowers, your favorite orange rolls from Lake Spark, and even something for our baby, and that one I think I nailed because it says *my little cupid*." He encourages me to step closer to him. "And I did all of that without answering my mom's hundredth call because she would probably berate me for not making a reservation somewhere."

I stutter a laugh. "You too?" Then it dawns on me. "Wait, did you say love?"

He knows he has me because of the wicked sexy smirk spreading. "I did."

"As in you are falling, meaning potentially love me?" I'm enjoying this conversation already.

"As in I *do* love you."

My bright smile hits my mouth like a firework. "Perfect then, because I love you too."

His intense eyes send me a message that this isn't a game. "It's kind of been obvious between us."

"It has." My heart is beating so fast. "I think I know a way that we can celebrate." I step back and purposely take my time to untie the belt of my robe to let it fall and pool at my feet, leaving me in my new lingerie.

Asher is instantly pleased, and he smacks his hand against the side of his cheek because I'm twisting his mind, heart, and cock in all directions. "Every time you do this to me, wear something like this, my thoughts go to places far dirtier than I thought I had. You are beautiful, I love you, and you're carrying my baby. I hope you realize that combination means I have every intention of living inside of you tonight."

I pout with fake disappointment. "But there are baked goods."

He storms forward and yanks me to his body, his hand fisting my hair in the back of my head. He has a savage look in his eyes. "The only way you are having cake is if I lick it off your body then kiss you."

Heat prickles my skin, and I feel the pounding of my clit. "That could get a little messy."

"As much as it could be fun, your little scraps of cloth need my attention. I won't let you get cold." Both of our eyes bounce down to my peaked nipples, then our gazes meet. "And I need to worship this body that has our baby growing inside of it." The tip of his fingers touch my belly. "Most of all, I need to make love to you slowly."

"Ooh, I like this Valentine's Day plan," I rasp.

He slams his mouth onto mine, and I'm certain this is my favorite Valentine's Day yet. Screw chocolates—okay, not the praline ones, but screw roses and teddy bears, because I have the best thing: a man who loves me and a baby on the way.

Our lips remain sealed as he guides me to where he wants

me. We only break our touch when we have to climb the stairs. The moment we both leave the top step, he winds me back to his body and glues our lips together.

When he lays me on the bed, we pause and get lost in one another's eyes. We are on the road that we are meant to be on.

We both attempt to recover as we stare at the ceiling. "Do you like Valentine's Day yet?"

He begins taking off his shirt and sweater. "It's sure as hell less stressful than Chrismukkah."

I giggle at his response, and it causes my chest to rise, which gives him an open canvas to kiss my chest. My hands comb through his hair to hang on, and my eyes close, as I'm in bliss.

# CHAPTER 18
## ASHER

I glare sidelong at my lovely baby mama. Gracie can't help it and giggles behind her pressed lips. We're sitting inside at a table dressed in pastels with an abundance of food in the middle.

"It's a serious matter. Your dad's version of an Easter egg hunt sent us all on a two-mile trek," I remind her.

"Not exactly two miles. More like the backyard, side yard, and front yard, but sure, we will say two miles."

My eyes grow bold. "And the speed boat that someone had to rowboat to?"

She is struggling not to give in to hysterical laughter. "*Technically,* the boat and that part of the lake is part of the backyard, right? Plus, it's for Drew's kids."

Shaking my head, I let it go. From the corner of my eye, I see the plate of matza next to the carrot cake that most definitely is filled with flour and everything that our grandparents would probably disapprove of. I internally cringe because nobody enjoys dry crackers, even if there is a sentiment behind it. I'm going to do this purely for tradition before I nosh on the giant piece of carrot cake.

I look around the table filled with family from both Gracie's and my side. It's Eastover. Because it is possible to mix Easter and Passover together when the calendar dates align.

"Your brother seems out of it, and I have the feeling he is up to something." Gracie seems to be reviewing the scene of Tyler and Shaw looking completely wrecked.

Yeah, the team arranged a trade, and Shaw ended up right under my nose on the bench. Not ideal, but I'm making it work.

I shift my gaze across the table and see Tyler about to fall asleep. A maintenance day for the team is needed. I rub my face and yawn. "Well, we do have one more week before playoffs. Not exactly low-adrenaline games. He probably just slept in. I barely made this. I have a window of opportunity before our next game, and I'm thankful that our families feel the speed version of the Seder reading is how we roll."

"I know, right?" she agrees.

Drew leans over the table to peek around Gracie and join the conversation. "How many years have we been doing this? I still don't know the story other than I'm about to drink a lot of wine and eat a bizarre radish."

"Least you get to drink the wine. I've resorted to grape juice," Gracie playfully complains right before she scoops up my hand from under the table and plants my palm against her belly.

This child started behaving last week and finally kicks when I'm around.

"So, how many times has my dad drilled you about a ring?" Drew wonders.

Gracie kicks his leg under the table, and he yelps. It's banter, the way siblings have.

My lips quirk out as I accept my fate that I'm going to be

roasted until this baby comes out and then every day after until the day comes where I present a ring.

"Yeah, when is that happening?" Shaw pipes up from across the table, more to tease me than anything.

I feel Gracie squeeze my hand on her belly because she is slightly tense. She hates when we are put on the spot. We are in no rush.

"My dad has been fine. Completely fine," Gracie proudly lies.

Hudson Arrows mentions it only about every time I see him. More in a future son-in-law wink kind of way.

"Gotta lock it in, Brother. As the wise man from Fiddler on the Roof would say: tradition." Why did someone decide to make him Tevye in his eighth-grade drama production? We never hear the end of it.

Drew lets out a deep laugh. "They skipped a step on that one."

When somebody clears their throat, I'm saved. All of our attention is given to the head of the table where my mom proudly stands, holding up the Seder book.

"Show of hands if we do the hour version with songs?"

The table stays quiet and not a single hand raised.

"And no songs, we use an app, and time this to a new record of forty minutes?"

Everybody raises their hand.

"Thought so." She smiles then sits down.

"One year when my great-grandmother was alive, it went on for four hours," Gracie whispers to me.

I lean into her, setting my arm on the back of her chair, and get a waft of her flowery shampoo. "Was a roasted lamb sacrificed for Easter dinner?"

Both of our eyes zip to the serving plate by Hudson. I'm

sure he was as overzealous with his cooking as his scavenger-hunt planning.

"We were lucky that year that Easter fell on an earlier date in the month," she explains. But then her eyes fixate on the piece of meat. "It's a little insensitive. It's baby lamb season. That thing on a plate was probably a parent. I can't think about it." Gracie sounds a tad somber, and it isn't in fun jest.

I also know where this is going.

Surveying the room, I see that everyone is still in their own conversations at the table before we begin. I have a moment.

I offer my hand as I stand. "Come on, let's get some air."

She nods in agreement while she stands.

When we walk down the hallways past the laundry room to the side door, she yanks me out, now eager for fresh air on a cloudy day. We nearly tumble into the side yard, but she releases my arm, and I step back, almost tripping on the croquet set that someone forgot to put away.

"I hate this game." I kick a wire tunnel.

"It involves a stick. Shouldn't it be like hockey on grass or something?

I wiggle a finger side to side. "No. This is the game for old people who move to Florida when they retire."

She rolls her eyes before a lightness hangs in the air. Remembering why I suggested we get some air, I step forward and ruefully smile as my finger hooks under her chin to drag her sight back to me.

"The lamb is really getting to you, huh?"

She laughs and cries at the same time. "So silly, I know. It's just a fluffy baby animal, and when I walked through the baby store, every toy and blanket had a little lamb on it. Hormones are getting to me."

My hand drops when she wraps her arms around my neck. "We're just getting closer to welcoming her. There's a lot going on. I don't think it's the lamb that is bothering you at all." I affectionately hold her eyes.

"No. It's not." Her voice softens. "It's becoming even more real that in a few months we're going to be parents."

"I think a lot more is becoming real." I mean us. Being with her drowns my soul because she's everything.

I stroke her cheek with the back of my knuckles, and the way our eyes lock feels like a silent agreement of the words we don't say aloud. There is a glint in her eyes, and the corner of her mouth tugs. "You're right," she rasps.

"I also think you miss me a little?" I'm teasing her, but I'm very much serious, too.

It is the faintest of nods, but I see it. "It's great the Spinners made it to the playoffs and all, mostly due to your leadership. It's just... it's hard. We knew it would be this way, barely a moment to breathe and traveling more until you qualify for the next round."

I smirk to myself and feel a little cocky because I'm positive that we will. But hockey doesn't matter right now. "Trust me, every moment I can, I think of you."

"We don't get many moments lately," she points out.

"True."

She quickly grabs my hand and directs it to her belly. "She's really moving today. I guess she knows that you're around." Gracie presses her lips together. It doesn't take a rocket scientist to see that she's struggling today.

A poke stomps against my hand, and her warm smile probably matches my own. "I'm very lucky to have you both." My lips feather her jawline, then I trail my mouth to nip on her lip. My feathery touch is abandoned when I kiss her deeply.

I can't get enough of her. Family is family, and they will play a big role in our little girl's life, but right now, I'm going to be selfish.

Struggling to pull away only to magnetize back to her, I manage to break our kiss and frame her face with my hands. "How about you fake that you are too tired, and we go pick up a pizza and head home? I could think of a few things that I would rather do right now."

She eases and sighs. "Perfect idea."

"Come on." I tip my head in the direction of the door.

We begin to walk, but then she pauses and snaps her fingers. "Oh yeah, now I remember that I solved a mystery at the table."

"What was what?"

Her smile is ear to ear, but it is disconcerting.

"What the hell is going on?" My brows rise, and I wait patiently for an answer.

"I overheard Lainey and Tyler whispering in the kitchen that your brother has totally been eyeing someone he really probably shouldn't be."

"Just tell me." My voice turns a little curt.

She shakes her head side to side, clearly entertained. "So, how good is the relationship going with Declan these days? It's good, right?" She's dragging this out.

"Come again?" My neck cranes as I connect the dots.

"You heard me."

My body begins to boil with tension. "Oh, I did, but allow me a few seconds of denial that my brother might fuck up his career by eyeing the team owner's daughter."

Now Gracie just laughs. "You know, our daughter will give you gray hairs when she is older, but right now, it seems your brother is filling that role."

"I'm going to fucking warn him."

She reaches out to tug my arm. "Relax. He hasn't done anything. Give him a reminder, keep it professional as Coach Tate, and look at yourself in the mirror right now because this is really kind of hilarious."

Shaking my head fervently side to side, I pinch the bridge of my nose. "Just get me out of here. I'm supposed to be relaxing you, but I might need to take a raincheck."

She interlinks our arms to lead us on our way. "Surely, you mean a reversal in positions." Her sultry voice already relaxes me.

"And this is why I love you."

"Because of my choice of sex positions?"

I gently nudge into her side. "A solid reason, but I meant it's your beautiful smile and witty words that have me excited for the future. You keep me grounded in this family of crazy too. It's a reason that I love you."

She rests her head on my shoulder. "I love you so much that I just got kicked hard because someone wants to remind me that she will get some of that love. It will be a different kind, but gosh, you have every inch of me."

Which is exactly why we are going home to lie in bed together.

# EPILOGUE: ASHER

## NEXT CHRISMUKKAH

This should be my quiet time. I have three days off for the Christmas break on the league schedule. I could just sit on the sofa cuddling with Talia for 72 hours straight. Maybe we would have guests stop by for an hour or two for coffee and cookies.

But no.

I'm at a table with Tyler, Lainey, Shaw, and the mother of my child. There are chocolate gold coins scattered around the table, and we're searching for the missing dreidel.

I'm smiling tightly, as Gracie's mom stole my child an hour ago to hold non-stop. I'll never see my daughter, who is dressed in a freaking reindeer onesie, again for the rest of the day. My mom has been waiting in the wings to swoop in like a hawk to take over when Talia starts to fuss. Gracie just affectionately glances at our family, happy that everyone is doting on our baby girl.

"The season is going strong," Hudson mentions as he peeks over my shoulder.

"Is it? I've contemplated spiking the eggnog with a little extra rum about three times in the last hour," I reply dryly.

"I meant the hockey season, not the holiday season. Your brother joining the team has really improved the power plays. Given Declan a few extra gray hairs, too."

"No kidding." I dread it.

Hudson presses his lips together to hide his pleased smile. "The holiday season is already exceptional since you are locking my daughter down with that ring coming her way."

Rolling my eyes, I don't want to be reminded of my brother and his reputation that he can't seem to shake.

Hudson walks away, and my father places his hand on my shoulder. "I'm kind of happy that we decided to cater this year's Christmas. Nobody cooking makes it more relaxed and gives us more time for fun." He hands me the missing dreidel. He's holding a scotch in his other hand because he values sanity.

"Chrismukkah," I correct him. "Piper and Mom will lose it if they hear anything less, and I'm positive Gracie's dead great-grandmother will haunt us at some point too."

"So true." He winks at me before walking away. My daughter giggles, and I check to see that Piper is bouncing her on her hip while they look at my daughter's first stocking hanging over the fireplace, with the menorah on the mantel.

Gracie claps her hands together and seems excited. "Let's get this drinking game going. I'm off mom duty, and I fully intend to take advantage of that."

I hand Gracie my dreidel, only for my brother to pounce in and steal it from her hand. "I call the blue one. It's my good luck color, and I need a Gimel to take it all."

Gracie just smiles, amused.

"No!" My instant panicked response causes everyone at the table to still and swing their attention to me.

Tyler and Lainey hide the smirk they both have. My brother and Gracie are truly puzzled.

I calm for a second. "I just mean, you don't want all of the chocolate. You have a game tomorrow. Plus, that was really rude. Give it back."

"What am I? Five? Really rude." He mocks me.

"Give it to Gracie," Tyler encourages.

Gracie touches my arm, still with an angelic smile on her face. "Relax, it's fine. I have no intention to actually play because who really knows the rules. Besides, I'm only here as an excuse to let loose. I don't care how it happens."

I scratch the back of my neck and roll my lips in, unsure of what to say or do.

Lainey seems to notice my predicament. "Give it to Gracie. Or I tell everyone how you've been eyeing the team owner's daughter," she grits out.

"Touchy. What is up with this game? Everyone seems so serious."

"Just give the dreidel to Gracie," my dad demands my brother from the sidelines. Great, let's add in a throwback to being a child to the night.

Gracie raises her hands. "What the hell is going on?

Suddenly it finally hits me what I'm about to do. I'm not nervous, I'm ready.

My brother seems to grasp that we are all imploring him to follow along. He slowly hands Gracie the dreidel, and his face screws up because he is trying to make sense of this situation.

"Spin it, and don't be gentle," I quietly implore the mother of our child.

The room is painfully quiet except for our daughter letting out a small coo.

Gracie keeps her eyes set on me and hesitantly accepts the

dreidel. She doesn't even blink once. Maybe she realizes what is about to happen.

Everyone here knows what is about to happen except the woman who a few seconds ago looked perplexed but now seems to grasp the situation. I asked for Hudson's permission at Thanksgiving, and then my dad helped me pick out the ring a few weeks ago. Call me traditional.

She sets the dreidel on the table and spins it. It feels as though everyone is holding their breath.

It lands on the table, and she studies it, trying to make sense, but then she sees it. A small crack. My cheeks tighten from a warm smile developing on my mouth. Her face blooms with a happiness that I haven't yet seen on her before.

She reaches down to touch the pieces that are broken and to shovel out the ring that is meant only for her.

She holds it up.

"*Ohhh*, that's why she needed the dreidel." My brother snaps his fingers. "Should have clued me in on this plan."

I don't give him even a glare, instead lolling my head to the side for a millisecond.

"Read the room. Shut up," Tyler mumbles to my brother and swats him.

Silence returns, with all eyes on us. This is my moment.

Sliding off my chair, I get down on one bent knee. "You'll always be the greatest holiday present. Will you marry me?"

Her face floods with emotion. Her eyes water and glisten, only making her more beautiful in this very moment.

"What the hell." Her eyes drop to the ring between her fingers.

My heart begins to pound so hard that I almost hear it in my ears, and I feel the room get smaller. Her eyes follow my every move.

"Are you crazy?" she nearly scolds me.

*What?* Oh shit.

I sweep my eyes across the room and see concerned faces.

"Asking you to marry me in a creative holiday way. How is that crazy?"

"The dreidel might never have broken, and then the ring would be stuck forever! Tell me this isn't my great-grandmother's ring that was passed down generations all the way back to when they lived on a Shtetel and the neighbor played a violin." She is dead serious.

I stare at her blankly. "That's Fiddler on the Roof, not your fifth-grade family genealogy report," I comment defensively.

"So full of wisdom, that movie." Shaw sets his hand on his heart.

Gracie holds my gaze for a second, and I'm reminded of how sharp she is. Because slowly the corner of Gracie's mouth begins to stretch because she's playing with me.

"Hmm, maybe I should hear the question again," she encourages and bites back her wide smile itching to escape.

*Phew.*

I interlink my fingers with her hand hanging low with the ring. "Gracie Arrows, will you marry me?"

Her eyes pierce through me and darts her love straight into my heart. "Yes. I'll be your wife."

Elation fills me, and my grin is wide. I stand to slip the ring on her finger, and the room erupts in noise and a mazel tov. Gracie throws her arms around my neck. "I'm going to be your wife." She kisses me, and I kiss her back with reverence that is respectable enough for the room.

The next few minutes are a blur. The kisses, the congratulations, the thumbs-up from my future father-in-law, and my brother grinning because he's happy for me and knows I will forgive him for ruining the scene… on several occasions.

I have a fiancée, the best gift, and I don't even think I was on Santa's nice list this year.

A few minutes later, one of the moms was kind enough to return our daughter into Gracie's arms because heaven forbid you get to hold your own child on a holiday.

I keep my hand on the small of Gracie's back as we admire the new ornaments on her parents' tree. She plays with Talia's hand and pretends to bite it. I look on, soaking in the scene.

She gushes over our daughter. "Our little girl's first Chrismukkah. A special time for our little cutie. This is a holiday for kids, and now that we have her, it just hits differently, you know?"

Reflecting for a second, I have to agree. "You're right."

"*And*." She throws me a teasing look. "We have a story to tell her because of her daddy's romantic skills."

I'm proud and maybe my face shows that.

Gracie steps closer. "Fiancé, how do you feel about Santa-themed sleeping attire? Light on the coverage front," she whispers with a sultry voice that only I can hear.

I cover Talia's ears with my hands. "Truthfully, it would kind of freak me out a bit. Naked works, though."

She giggles under her breath, her eyes taunting me. "Thank goodness that we think alike because I ditched the Santa idea and opted for the classic winter colors in satin for later."

"Gosh, you're meant for me." I dive in to steal a kiss from her plump and soft lips.

"Nah, really meant for you would be me telling you that I made sure my mom added extra rum to my dad's favorite yule log."

"Lucky that I'm marrying my soulmate then."

She smiles with a shade of agreement on her face before stealing a kiss from me.

In the back of my head, I remember how this all started. I'm used to the blue lines on the ice deciding the fate of a play. Two lines on a pregnancy test decided my fate for life. There were no boundaries, but I knew exactly where I stood. It was then I looked into Gracie's eyes, and I knew that a slapshot had just hit my heart.

We were unexpectedly thrown together. And now every holiday season only seems to get better with her.